Weirdo's War

Weirdo's War

Michael Coleman

Orchard Books : New York

First American edition 1998 published by Orchard Books
First published in Great Britain in 1996 by Orchard Books London

Orchard Books, 95 Madison Avenue, New York, NY 10016

Manufactured in the United States of America
Book design by Vicki Fischman
The text of this book is set in 12 point Janson.
10 9 8 7 6 5 4 3 2

Library of Congress Cataloging-in-Publication Data
Coleman, Michael, date.
Weirdo's war / by Michael Coleman. — 1st American ed.
p.   cm.
Summary: While trapped in a cave with one of his fellow students, a
longtime enemy, Daniel relives his troubled relationship with his schoolmates.
ISBN 0-531-30103-6 (trade : alk. paper).
ISBN 0-531-33103-2 (lib. bdg. : alk. paper)
[1. Schools—Fiction. 2. Interpersonal relations—Fiction. 3. Caves — Fiction.]
I. Title.
PZ7.C67716We 1998 [Fic]—dc21 98-10482

For J. W. and all the "Southampton Explorers"

"I am the way I am. That's the way I'm made."

—*Jacques Prévert*

—

"Making peace is harder than making war."

—*Adlai Stevenson*

Chapter 1

From the moment the ground gave way beneath our feet, it couldn't have taken more than a couple of seconds. But it seemed to go on forever, a nightmare in slow motion.

"Watch out. It's slippery in here."

I followed him into the cave, the entrance just a thin slit in the rock.

Out of the wet and into the dry. Out of the warm and into the cool. Out of the light and into the dark.

That's when it happened. I heard the groan of the earth. A shout. The sound of him falling. And then it was as if somebody had pulled the ground from beneath my feet and I was falling too.

I didn't scream.

Funny. I remember that quite clearly. I didn't scream as I fell. Just found myself wondering how far it was to the bottom, and how fast I'd be going when I got there.

Then thinking: they're right. They're right, all of them.

I *am* a weirdo.

Apart from a few bruises, I'm not injured. Neither is Tozer.

As instructed, I've been blowing my whistle. Tozer's is lost, of course.

Instead, he's been playing his flashlight beam over the glistening walls as if he's hoping it will burn a hole through the rock. Correction: the *limestone* rock. I know that for a fact.

Once more he shines the beam of light on the floor of this place. Then, quickly, he switches it away and up, up toward where we came in.

The beam isn't strong enough to penetrate the blackness. All I can make out, high above us, is the thin shaft of light that's squeezing through the rock and slime now blocking the entrance.

No way out, I hear in my head.

I blow my whistle again, listening until the shriek fades and dies as if it's been soaked up by the limestone all around us.

Nothing. No shouts, no calls. No indication that anybody out there has heard us. Nothing.

Tozer clicks his flashlight off. I hear him take a deep breath. Then, in the black silence, he says, "You scared, Daniel?"

You scared? How many times have you said that to me, Tozer? Dozens? Hundreds, even.

But this time it's different.

He hasn't called me "Weirdo," for a start.

He's called me by my proper name. I can't remember the last time he did that. Ten years ago? When we were both four or five and starting school together?

But we're not at school. He isn't towering over me in some distant corner of the school grounds asking, "You scared, Weirdo?"

He hasn't got me in a headlock, with one of his powerful hands wrenching my arm up behind my back so that it's all I can do to stop myself screaming with the pain. He isn't forcing me to bow before his great friends, Greg and Flick, as they stand there, loving the show.

No. We're here, under the ground. With no way out.

Tozer asks again, "Eh? You scared?"

It sounds as if he wants to make sure I'm still here. I don't suppose he can see me. In the blackness I can't see him. It's like we're blind.

The sensation switches my mind into gear. My weirdo uncontrollable mind, which thinks thoughts and raises questions even though I'm begging it to stop.

You've got five senses, Daniel. If you're blind, that's one down. What are the other four telling you? Smell. What can you smell?

I can smell the damp in here. I can't describe it. But I can smell it.

What can you hear?

I can hear the damp too. Little drops, plopping into puddles somewhere. And echoing. As if it's raining indoors.

Touch?

I reach out my hand and feel the wall of wet limestone rock, slippery and rough at the same time.

Taste, Daniel. Can you taste anything?

Oh, yes. I admit it. I can taste something. Something I can't mistake. I've known it often enough. It's a taste that comes up from somewhere inside me, squeezing my chest on its way, like a traveling hand.

The taste of fear.

I've known it from the boy sitting with me now, in this place. And it's now that I give Tozer the answer I've never let him have the pleasure of hearing before.

"Yes, I am. I'm scared."

In the darkness I imagine the slow, dumb grin spreading across his face. Slow and dumb because, let's be honest, that's the sort of brain Tozer's got. As slow and dumb as mine is quick and uncontrollable.

So in my mind's eye I see him grinning.

I'm wrong.

He makes a noise. At first I can't work out what it is; I just know it isn't a laugh.

Suddenly I realize he's crying. Tozer's crying— softly, as if he's never done it before and he's not sure if he's doing it the right way.

"Oh, no," he moans.

He's trying to stop his fear from getting out, but he can't. "I'm really scared," he sobs, his voice cracking. "What are we going to do?"

Even now, as I start whistling for help again, I can't keep my mind under control. I hear Tozer crying and what does it do? Flashes a stupid joke up for me, that's all.

When did Daniel Edwards begin to see Tosh Tozer in a new light? When they were stuck underground in the pitch dark together. . . .

Chapter 2

It's not as if we'd ever been friends. Not that you'd have expected us to be. We'd always been as different as chalk and cheese.

Why chalk and cheese? Why not chalk and chips? Chimneys and cheese? Zebras and xylophones?

But, for all that, Tozer had moved in and out of my life over the years. Not often, but enough. A bit like a bad dream that comes back again just when you think you've got over it.

I first became aware of him at elementary school. Mind you, it would have been hard not to be aware of him. From the day he started, Tozer was bigger than almost everybody else. And, whether he knew it or not, he used that fact. If ever there was a game of something going on Tozer would be there, bulldozing his way through it.

Me? I didn't want to know, even then.

Give me the chance and I'd stay inside, drawing shapes and patterns or decorating my worksheets in fantastic colors. Or making lists. Lists of things I'd seen on the way to school. Lists of buildings. Lists of animals. Lists of trees. Lists of cars—makes, colors, styles.

I'd devise bar charts, drawing them, coloring them in, looking for patterns or wondering why there weren't any, until . . .

"Daniel Edwards, how many more times do you have to be told? Go on, go outside. Get some fresh air."

That was the usual.

It was on one of those days that, you might say, Tozer first made his mark on me.

We'd been learning about endangered species. I was in the middle of making yet another of my famous lists when the "get some fresh air" command came.

Outside, there was a game of baseball going on. They'd set up bases with their school caps and were using an old tennis racquet and ball. Tozer was in the thick of things as usual, complaining that his team was a player short and defying the others to start the game before the sides were even.

Before I knew it he'd spotted me. Until that day, I don't think he'd really noticed me. We'd been in different classes, different groups, different worlds. I was dragged into the game, and all that ended.

The memory's as clear as if it was yesterday. The game starts. We field first. Tozer orders me to stand at second base.

He goes behind, to play catcher. He isn't very

good. A couple of the quicker-witted kids aim some comments at him from a safe distance, raising a few laughs. Then, somehow, the ball's hit into the bushes, which edge the end of the playground.

Tozer blunders in after it. As the bushes shake, the endangered species lesson pops back into my mind.

"It's a wild rhino!" I yell.

It was the first time I'd ever made any of them laugh. Around me, others start making gorilla hoots and elephant bellows. Tozer must have heard it all. The moment he comes out of the bushes he looks my way.

"Catch, Danny!"

He's lobbed the tennis ball in my direction. At least, I think it's the tennis ball. But it isn't. It's an old baseball he's found in there—moldy, covered in muck, but still very hard.

It hits me smack in the mouth.

I screamed bloody murder of course. I didn't do it to get him in trouble, but it did. He got a letter home and, I learned later, a belting from his dad.

Me? I got a busted front tooth. Mom oohed and aahed and said she'd take me to the dentist and have it made as good as new. Dad said it wasn't worth the bother; it was a baby tooth and it would fall out soon anyway.

"It makes you look tough, Danny," he told me.

I checked. I remember noticing that the missing bit

was shaped like a triangle, with one side slightly longer than the other.

But I don't ever remember thinking it looked tough. It didn't feel tough. For the best part of a year, all that triangular shape did was to remind me of Tosh Tozer every time I looked in the mirror. When it did finally loosen and come out, I dropped it on the ground and stamped on it until it had no shape left at all.

Tozer and I started at Ferneham High on the same day. Months earlier, when she thought I was asleep in bed, Mom had made noises about sending me to Grove Manor, a private school.

From the way his voice pierced the bedroom floor-boards it was pretty clear that Dad didn't agree.

"Grove Manor! Margaret, do you know what they charge at that place?"

"I know it would be expensive, Gary. We'd have to make sacrifices. But they'd bring out the best in him there."

A snort. "The only thing they'd bring the best out of would be my wallet!"

"But he's bright, Gary," says Mom. Her voice alters, growing uncertain. "I think he might be gifted."

"Gifted!"

I look out of my bedroom door and down into the living room just as Dad flings his newspaper on the sofa and fixes Mom with one of his no-messing stares.

"He's got no friends, love. He doesn't mix with other kids. Going to a stuck-up place like Grove Manor is the last thing he needs."

"He does mix." Mom's on the defensive. She's losing, and I reckon she knows it. "He goes to the swimming club, doesn't he?"

"And does what? Says nothing to anybody, just swims up and down, up and down, till it's time to get out."

"So, he's quiet."

"Quiet!" The newspaper's being retrieved. "Margaret, he's antisocial. That's what he is."

They sit in silence for a few minutes. Finally Mom gives him the opening he's waiting for.

"You think Ferneham is the best idea then?"

He doesn't even lower the newspaper. It's as if the sports page is pronouncing the final word on my future.

"Yes, I do. Let him go mix with normal kids, Margaret. That's what he needs."

So I went to Ferneham, a mile down the road and free of charge, to mix with normal kids like Tozer.

Now, when I say "mix" I mean mix in the way that a lottery machine mixes its numbered balls. That's what you are, a numbered ball, you and everybody else. You're tossed in, the air starts blowing, and away you go, up and down, around and around. And who do you come out with? Well, that's the lottery bit.

So Tozer and I went in, and the Ferneham mixer did its stuff.

He came out with Greg Yeandle and Flick Harris. Greg Yeandle, good at most things, and well aware of it. Flick Harris, just aware—of fads and fashions, who was wearing what, doing what. Called Flick on account of him being the only ninth grader who wanted to comb his hair rather than simply let it happen.

For most of that first year I saw little of Tozer. When I did, I almost felt sorry for him.

He always seemed to be the odd man out, ignored, just tagging along behind Greg and Flick like an over-size pet poodle. Or, if they were taking any notice of him, it was because he was amusing them by making himself look stupid.

And what did the Ferneham mixer do with Daniel Edwards?

Not a lot, is the answer to that. I went in on my own and came out on my own. Maybe that's what attracted Tozer's attention to me again.

It was then I got the "Weirdo" tag.

For some reason, Ferneham has its library on the top floor of the school's main building, otherwise known as A-Block. Maybe it was put up there to deter those who only wanted a laze on the school's softest seats. If so, the strategy worked. I soon discovered that the library was rarely crowded and often empty.

Perfect, as far as I was concerned. I could do my homework, read my books, do what I wanted.

Until one day, it wasn't empty.

Tozer was in there, his feet up on a table. Beside him, Greg and Flick had books in front of them.

I sat down in my usual spot, on the other side of the library. Tozer glanced my way. I saw him lean across and say something to the other two. They looked over as well.

The next thing I know, Greg Yeandle is standing at my shoulder.

"Tosh reckons you've probably done that math homework," he says. It's the first time he's ever spoken to me.

"Does he?"

"He does." Greg looks over at Tozer. "Isn't that right, Tosher? You think Danny-boy here might have done the math?"

Tozer nods, like a puppet.

"He reckons you're a mathematical genius, does Tosher."

"He likes the stuff." Tozer let his feet fall to the floor with a thump, then lumbers over. "I mean, he actually *likes* the stuff. Real weirdo, he is."

"Weirdo, eh?" Greg studies me. He smiles, without showing his teeth. "He doesn't look like a weirdo, Tosh. He looks normal enough."

"Maybe he's bionic?" calls Flick. He's got his comb

out, sliding it through his hair. "Got a computer for a brain, has he, Tosh?"

"Yeh. More'n likely."

"That true, Danny-boy?" asks Greg. More smile but still no teeth.

What could I say? Yes? No? I didn't know the answer myself. Still don't. All I knew was that it'd always been that way.

Numbers have always had a special fascination for me—the way they form, the way they repeat, the way you can mix them and use them, mold them like a potter molds a lump of clay.

Questions would buzz in and out of my mind.

Is the shortest distance between two points always *a straight line?*

It looks like it should be. You can draw diagrams on the ground and step the distances out to show that it's so—for that diagram. But how do you know it's the case for every possible diagram that could be drawn?

Do three angles of every *triangle add up to 180 degrees?*
Why, why, why? Can it be proved?

Can you work out the speed a stone is going if you know how far it's fallen?
How?

Can equations be used to describe everything? The curve of a bridge? The thrust of a rocket? How about the flight of a swallow?

Greg eases his leg onto the corner of the table.

When he speaks, he sounds as though he's being friendly.

"How about giving us a little look, then? I'm just a bit stuck on number fourteen."

"And sixteen," Flick calls over.

"Go find your own help," says Greg.

"Oh, please!" Flick falls to his knees, clamping his hands together in mock prayer. "Please, please, please. *Please*, Danny-boy. The one about the polygon."

"What's parrots got to do with anything?" says Greg, automatically. Standard joke.

Tozer laughs. Standard laugh, like it was one of his duties.

Greg changes his tone. Sugarcoated now. "Come on, Daniel. It won't hurt. Just a look. You won't feel a thing, I promise."

So, what would you have done? Handed your book over for them to copy from? Ah, but you're not me. Nobody is.

"Look," I say, "they're quite easy. I'll show you how to do them."

"Just show us your book," says Greg. "That's easiest for us. Right, Tosh?"

It's the signal. Before I can do anything to stop him, Tozer leans over and snatches my bag. He tosses it to Greg sideways, as if it's a football.

"Give that back!" I yell. "Give that back!"

Pathetic, really. And a waste of breath. Greg has

already snapped open the catch and is shuffling through everything.

That's what gets to me. Into my head, drumming faster and faster, one thought.

That bag's organized, and he's messing it all up!

Maybe neither of them expected me to go for him, otherwise I'd never have got past Tozer as easily as I did. But before Greg Yeandle knows it I'm on him, grabbing his wavy hair and yanking his head back. He gives a yelp of pain and lets my bag drop.

It's all right now. He's not messing it up anymore.

It's enough for me. I step back as he turns around.

"Okay, Danny-boy," says Greg as I clutch my bag tight. His scowl melts slowly into his no-teeth smile. "Okay—Weirdo."

Behind him, still in his seat on the other side of the room, Flick is smiling too. He's seen what I haven't—that Greg is holding something behind his back.

I turn away.

Then I hear Yeandle say, "Well now, what have we got here?"

I know at once what he's got, what he's taken from my bag. The one thing I don't want him—anybody—to see.

This time I don't dash in. The folder he's taken out is too valuable. Too, too valuable. It shows in my voice.

"Look. That won't interest you. It's mine. It's—a hobby."

Greg is thumbing through the pages, pausing, sniffing, turning it upside down for effect. Tozer laughs obediently. He takes it over and shows it to Flick. Flick looks at it pop-eyed, his nose touching the pages.

"Veeerrrry impressive."

"Very," says Greg, head nodding slowly.

For a moment I think he's serious. I relax slightly, half of me still fearful, the other half pleased that anybody should have shown an interest in what they'd seen.

"Really?"

"Really," says Greg.

"They're just calculations," I say. "I do them for fun."

"I can see that, Daniel."

He's interested. He's really interested.

"Look. I've worked out how tall all the school buildings are. There's a page for each of them."

"You don't say?"

Greg turns the folder toward me, to show a page headed A-Block. In a box there are my calculations and the result. One hundred fifty feet high. Beneath the box there's another maze of numbers.

He points at them. "What's this lot about, then?"

Still I don't get it, just ramble on, thinking he's really interested in what I'm telling him.

"Remember we did gravity in science last week? How it makes things accelerate toward the ground when you drop them? I've worked out a formula for how fast something would go if you dropped it from the top of any of the school buildings. It's simple. You just multiply the height by the gravity constant—you know, the one Mr. Redrow mentioned—double it, then take the square root . . ."

"Really? So something dropped from the top of this building would hit the ground at . . ." He looks at the result at the bottom of the page. "Sixty miles an hour?"

"Yes. Amazing, isn't it?"

"It certainly is, Danny-boy." He hands the open folder across to Tozer. "What do you reckon, Tosh? Reckon something dropped from this building would hit the deck at sixty?"

That slow, dumb grin spreads slowly across Tozer's face. But, slow as he is, he's still managed to get the message faster than me.

Not until Tozer says, "Only one way to find out, boss," and turns toward the window, do I finally realize what's happening.

"No. No, don't. Please . . ."

The library windows weren't designed to open very wide. Not enough to let an average-sized student slip through, anyway. But a ring binder? Yes, wide enough for a ring binder.

"Please!"

It's no use. Before I'm halfway across to him, Tozer has snapped open the rings and thrust the binder upside down out of the window.

Helplessly, I watch the pages flutter out, twisting and turning as they fall. Some go one way, some another. On the ground, faces turn up to see what's happening, laughing as the sheets spiral down toward them.

"Well, what do you know?" says Flick, coming over to watch. "Loose leaves. It must be autumn."

He laughs. Tozer laughs, though I'm not sure he knows what at. Yeandle just smiles.

Me, I can't—won't—make a sound. I just know from that moment I'll never beg them for mercy again.

As the last page flutters away, Tozer pulls my binder back in through the window. He tosses it back to me, pleased with himself, a servant who's finished a job well done.

Greg shakes his head. "Those pages definitely weren't going at sixty, Danny-boy," he says. "Got your sums wrong, I reckon . . ."

It took me the best part of an hour to find my precious pages.

Most were lying on the grass beneath the library. Some had reached the playground, where feet had stamped on them and bike wheels been ridden across them. A couple were under the wooden seats on the far side.

One, the last one, had even reached the tennis courts. I found it clinging to the wire fence like a bat.

And as I searched, what was I thinking? Was I ranting and raving, calling down curses on Tosh Tozer and

Greg Yeandle and Flick Harris and my weak-willed mom and pigheaded dad and anybody else I could think of?

No.

I was wondering if Greg Yeandle was right, and I really had got my sums wrong.

No, you haven't. Pages flutter, get slowed down by the wind. But a brick wouldn't. A brick would have hit the ground at sixty.

And then I'm wondering how things would have to change to take the wind into account and whether I could have worked out a formula to predict where my pages had ended up.

I'm actually feeling quite happy.

Weird, eh?

Chapter 3

"They—they'll come and look for us, won't they?"

I nod, then remember that in the blackness Tozer can't see me.

"Bound to."

"You know, send out a search party? When we don't come back?"

"Of course they will. We've just got to wait, that's all."

Tozer lets out a shuddering sigh, as if he's cried all he can. "I don't know if I can *stick it*. Just sitting here . . ."

"We'll have to," I say. "That's what it says in the instructions."

"Stuff the instructions," growls Tozer.

I hear him get to his feet, hear the solid clump of his boots on the rock and earth of the floor. He clicks on his flashlight again. In the arc of light I can see his waterproof jacket, streaked with mud. One elbow's been ripped open, and the pale gray of his sweatshirt is peeping through.

As he aims the flashlight upward I see his face. That's muddy, too, but smudged clean around his eyes from where he's rubbed the tears away with the backs of his hands.

"Anyway," I say, logical as ever, "we *can't* move, can we?"

He doesn't speak, just stands there for a few seconds breathing hard and playing the light around our limestone dungeon. The walls are almost sheer, encircling us. It's like we're at the bottom of a tall, rough-sided cylinder of rock.

A cylinder. Volume equals radius squared, times constant pi, times the height of the cylinder.

High up, far out of reach, there's still the faint sliver of light from where we came in.

How high? Twenty feet? How wide? Thirteen feet? Volume equals about twenty-seven-hundred cubic feet. Who cares? Shut up!

"One of us could move," says Tozer, "if there was a way out. Go for help."

"You know what we were told. No solo acts."

"Who cares what we were told! We were told to come in here, weren't we!"

As Tozer shouts, he swings the flashlight beam down to the floor, keeping it steady, trying to control himself.

"We just have to stay put," I say as calmly as I can. "When they realize we're missing, they'll come looking for us."

Tozer's waterproof jacket rustles as he sits down again. He switches off his flashlight once more.

Suddenly, as if he's in the dining hall at school, he says, "Got anything to eat?"

I push a hand into the left-hand pocket of my backpack, fingers searching for the solid oblong of chocolate I know is there. I snap the bar in half.

"Chocolate," I say, adding, "*dark* chocolate."

No reaction. The joke's lost on Tozer. I can't tell them the way Flick does.

I reach out toward him, stretching until my hand bumps against the slimy, muddy front of his jacket. His hand finds mine, then fumbles the chocolate away.

"Thanks," he murmurs, his mouth already full.

He munches on, the crinkling of silver paper the only sound I can hear above the constant drip, drip, drip of water.

Then suddenly he says, "Why'd you do this?"

"Do what?"

"This school trip. Why'd you come on it? Eh? Nobody had to. Wouldn't have thought it was your thing."

"It isn't my thing. *That's* why I'm here."

I can almost see the cloud pass across his face. "Come again?"

"This week . . . the exercises, the teamwork business, the outdoor stuff. It isn't my sort of thing. I'd have hated it even without—"

I stop as my mind goes on.

Even without you, Tozer. You and the rest of them.

I don't have to say it. He knows it well enough. I just go on with what I'd meant to say. "Anyway. I've hated most of it. Just like I knew I would. Just like *he* knew I would."

"He?"

"My dad. He's the reason I'm here. He said it would do me good . . ."

—

I'd argued, of course I had. I'd tried every word-twisting, argumentative trick in the book. Nothing had worked.

So, my dad doesn't find me easy. I know that.

He's a mixer, see? Life and soul of the party, always meeting and greeting. That's what makes it so hard for him. He doesn't—maybe he can't—understand how anybody could actually enjoy being on their own, could actually prefer it.

But I do. I don't need people around me. Silence is great. You can hear yourself think when it's quiet.

Anyway, I brought the letter home in the middle of the fall semester. It read like something an adman had dreamed up.

WORKING TOGETHER—an educational opportunity for your son during the spring break. Learning to work as a valuable member of a team in the delightful surroundings of the Combe Warren Center in the Mendip Hills.

It went on to describe the delights of spending five days tramping the hills and countryside and five nights of sleeping it off in a wooden hut.

There was no way I wanted to go, but there was no way of hiding the letter either. Ferneham—distrustful or, more likely, knowing the sort of kids they're dealing with—always have a reply slip at the bottom of their letters. No reply and it's another letter asking why no reply.

What happens if that one doesn't get a reply?

Still, I wasn't too worried. It meant paying out some money, after all, and Dad was never keen on that. So there it sat, in the rack on the kitchen wall. Mom and Dad didn't mention it, and neither did I.

Then Christmas came.

You know the sort of thing. House full of people. Hazily remembered aunts and uncles on their annual visit. Endless "Ooh, hasn't he grown?" and talking about you as if you're not there.

I survived Christmas Day itself—just. I'd got what I asked for, a diver's watch, one I could wear in the swimming pool. Stacks of functions and water resistant to 150 feet. Twiddling with that saw me through. But, by the next day, I'd had enough.

I went down to the pool. It was beautiful, almost empty. Me and the lifeguard most of the time. And, when he got bored, just me.

A few lengths, slow and leisurely, thinking, thinking.

How is it that a lump of steel sinks, but umpteen thousand tons of ocean liner manage to float?

And then, down to the deep end to test my watch. Diving to the bottom, checking that the second hand's still going around. Water resistant to 150 feet, so seven should be no problem.

Then, seeing how long I could hold my breath underwater. Trying again, seeing if I could stay under for longer this time. Doing it again, taking on the challenge, aiming for a personal best.

One more time. Waiting for the second hand to come around to zero. Deep breath. Under. Down to the bottom. Watching the second hand move onward.

You can do it.

Watching. Eyes closing with the effort. Opening again. The second hand has stopped. No, it hasn't. But it's moving so slowly.

Keep going. You can do it.

The strain. I've got to come up. I've got to.

Nearly there. Hold on. Nearly there. Done it!

Lungs bursting. Now I can go up.

Wait. Wait. Another five seconds. See if you can.

I wait. And wait. Suddenly, it's no effort anymore. There's no strain. The pounding in my ears has gone. It's peaceful down here. So peaceful . . .

Mom and Dad had only just realized I wasn't at home when the hospital telephoned. I caught snatches of the conversation they had with the nurse in the corridor.

"Don't worry, he'll be fine . . . the lifeguard pulled him out in time, pumped the water out of him . . . he'd only turned his back for a minute . . . God knows what the boy was trying to do . . . could have killed himself . . . we'll keep him in tonight, if there are no after-effects he'll be able to go home tomorrow . . ."

Mom stayed the night, wringing her hands and crying a lot. Dad stayed for a while, then went back to the guests.

While he was at the hospital he said hardly anything, just looked upset. By the next day, though, his mood had hardened. When I got back home the first thing I saw was the school trip letter. He'd taken it from the rack. It was spread out on the table. And signed.

"You're going on this, Daniel," he said.

"I don't want to."

"Gary . . ."

"Margaret, I've had enough. If this trip teaches him anything about getting on with other kids then it'll be worth every penny."

"I don't want to go," I say again.

"You are *going*! Understand? You're going! It'll do you good."

—

In the darkness I hear a disbelieving laugh.

"Your old man said that to you?" says Tozer. "'It'll do you good'? He really said that to you?"

"Really. Yes."

"Funny."

The way he says it, I can tell he's shaking his head.

"What's funny about it?"

"I'll tell you what's funny about it. You know what my old man said to me when I took that letter home?"

"What?"

"'You can go on this,' he said. 'A week with you out of the way—it'll do *me* good.' Get it?"

"I get it."

Silence, as though he's thinking. Then he says, "Has it?"

"Has it what?"

"Done you any good?"

Tozer's asking me that? After the week we've had, he's asking me that?

"What do you think?"

I hear the rustle of his jacket as he shrugs.

"Dunno." He forces out a laugh, scared and bitter at the same time. "Maybe we should ask Axelmann, eh?"

Axelmann.

As Tozer spits out that name it seems to echo around the walls.

Axelmann, Axelmann, Axelmann.

It's the name of the one thing the two of us have *really* got in common.

Chapter 4

"My name's Jeff Axelmann . . ."

He smiled broadly at our surprise that he should actually tell us his first name, rather than the usual "mister" we'd had from all the other teachers during the start-of-school-year introduction rituals. I could see bets going around about who would call him "Jeff" first.

". . . and as a reward for surviving your first year at Ferneham, you've got me for P.E. this year."

A ripple of laughter. More sideways looks. Was I the only one who thought that what he really meant was, "You've got me for P.E. this year, and aren't you lucky?"

He was chewing gum. As he chewed he examined us. Chew, look. Chew, look. He took his time—which gave us plenty of time to examine him, of course.

Casually swept-back hair that must have taken ages to get just right. Broad shoulders, encased in a steel-colored jogging-suit top. Short, stocky legs, which he flexed as he spoke, like he was warming up for something.

He looked athletic. He *was* athletic. That's what he wanted us to be quite clear about.

Chew. "And I'm sure we're all going to enjoy ourselves"—chew, chew, friendly looking grin—"or else."

Smiles all around. Axelmann sounded friendly.

And, for a while, he was. If he met any of us around school he'd wink and say something like, "All right?" He even did it to me once. It didn't last.

As the term wore on, an Axelmann "all right?" became like a gold star, only awarded to those he'd discovered were good at sports. The rest of us he ignored.

Well, I say the rest of us.

I was in that group for a while.

Tozer never was.

If I'm honest, Tozer was unlucky. If it hadn't been him it would have been somebody else. Tozer just happened to be the one who caught Axelmann's eye first.

We were in the gym, playing one of Axelmann's fun games. He calls it "Race to the Roof." A relay race, with everybody having to climb the wall bars, touch the ceiling, then come down and hand off to the next person on your team.

The race starts. We're in two teams, and it's neck and neck all the way. Even I manage to get up and down without a disaster. Not fast, but not so slow that Axelmann notices me.

Finally, only the last pair is left. Tozer on their side, Greg Yeandle on ours.

Tozer charges across the gym. Whether to impress Axelmann, or because he knows he's got to do something special to beat Greg, I don't know, but from the look on his face it's obvious he's really trying.

Launching himself onto the wall bars, Tozer starts climbing like crazy. Halfway up, he's actually in the lead. By the time he's reached the top, though, Greg's caught him. They touch the ceiling together and start to come down again.

That's when Tozer slips.

It's no great surprise in a way because he's not a natural mover like Greg and is stretching for all he's worth. But the result is that one moment he's clambering down, the next he's throwing out a hand looking for the wall bars—anything—to stop himself falling off altogether.

Nearby, the climbing ropes have been gathered together and tethered to a hook on the wall. They're what Tozer grabs.

It's only for a couple of seconds, but for that time it looks like he's swinging through the jungle on a trail of vines as he sways between the ropes and the wall bars. Finally he steadies himself enough to get both hands back on the wall bars. By now, Greg's down and home.

As I say, it could have happened to anybody. If it had, then that person would have been Axelmann's target—the one he picks on whenever he's losing the class's attention and wants to get it back again. But it didn't happen to anybody; it happened to Tozer.

"Six point zero for artistic impression, son." Axelmann laughs as Tozer finally puffs back to his spot. "Reckon I'll have to call you Monkey from now on."

And he has.

Whenever the class needs quieting down, it's: "Stop chattering, Monkey."

Or, when he wants to get everybody looking his way, it's: "Right, face the front, you lot. Monkey, stop scratching."

It works too. The class always laughs.

Including me.

And including Tozer.

That's what I can't understand. Tozer always laughs too.

Me and Axelmann? That came a couple of months later.

Until then, he hadn't noticed me at all. No great surprise, really. When it comes to sports, I'm pretty anonymous.

The trouble started on the day I wasn't. We'd just come back after midterm. The schedule had changed, as schedules do. Instead of galloping around in the gym, we'd switched to soccer.

Now, don't get me wrong. I don't mind soccer. I enjoy watching it a lot. There's a lot of math in soccer. Geometry, for instance. The way good teams pass the ball around in little triangles, and the way goalkeepers position themselves to give a forward the smallest angle to shoot at.

Then there's the way outfield players will set their bodies at different angles so as to make the ball stay on the ground or float or spin. I've often wondered if it's possible to come up with an equation to describe the curve of a perfect free kick.

But playing soccer on a freezing cold morning—which is what we were being asked to do that day—sorry, but I don't see the point.

My mistake was to say as much to Axelmann.

"Run around, run around," he's yelling. "Get warmed up."

Okay, maybe it was my fault. But when somebody tells me to do something, I like to know why—especially when I'm shivering in a pair of shorts and regulation school sports shirt and he's done up like an Arctic explorer.

So I say, "If we were in the gym we *would* be warm."

Axelmann looks at me as if he's seeing me for the first time. He gives his ever-present gum a couple of chomps. "And you are?" he says finally.

"Daniel Edwards." I think of adding, "Jeff," but he doesn't give me time.

"Well cut out the funnies, Edwards," he snaps, "and start moving."

He punts a ball up into the air and yells to the world at large, "Colors v. Whites. Fifteen minutes each way!"

I don't move.

"Why do we have to do this?"

Axelmann doesn't even look at me, just watches the ball return to earth as he says, "Because it's on the schedule."

In my head a little bell goes ping.

Sensible question, silly answer.

"Does the schedule say we have to do it outdoors?"

This time Axelmann does look at me. "What?" Chew.

"It might say soccer on the schedule, but does it say *outdoors*?"

"No, it doesn't. But it's good for you."

Sensible questions—two. Silly answers—two.

"Why?" I ask.

"Because it gets you out of a stuffy, centrally heated classroom and puts some fresh air into your lungs, that's why."

"We can open a window and do that."

Now Axelmann's looking at me as if I'm stupid. "Well that won't get your blood circulating around your little system, will it? Unlike running, which is healthy."

I point. Most of the class are standing in groups shivering, while the good soccer players are just passing the ball to each other. "So how many of us are running, sir? Six out of thirty? Twenty percent?"

Axelmann stops chomping. It's a sure sign I'm getting to him, but I don't stop.

"Why don't we just run, then? Why do we have to chase around after a bag filled with air? Why can't we just run? Indoors. You could time us. We could try and beat a personal best or something. That would encourage *everybody*. There'd be some point in that."

Still he tries to fob me off with any old answer.

"We do that, Edwards," he says. He's given up the tough stuff. Now it's heavy sarcasm. "We call it track. T-r-a-c-k. Understand? We do it in the spring."

"In the spring? When it's warm?"

"What?"

I can see he doesn't know what to say. I go on, twisting and turning the logic for the fun of it.

"So you don't let us get warm in the winter by running, because we get warm in the spring by running— which is the time of year when we don't need to get warm because it's warm then anyway. Is that what you're saying, Mr. Axelmann?"

It has to happen, of course.

"All right, Edwards," he snaps. "That's enough. You do it because *I* say so. Got that?"

Because I say so. The last throw of the person who's run out of arguments. You do it, not because I can convince you it's right, but because I say so.

The winner—Daniel Edwards!

I salute. "Yes, sir!"

I run off, elated at winning the battle of the minds.

He gave out the letters about the school trip at the end of that lesson.

"One for you, Brains—just to prove I can count that high."

It was the way he said it, lips tight and eyes cold.

Only then did it occur to me that, though I'd won our battle, the war had just begun.

Chapter 5

Tozer flicks his flashlight on. It flares brightly for an instant, then sinks to a tired glow.

"Your batteries are going," I say.

He shrugs. "So? Sitting here in the dark's driving me up the wall."

He doesn't realize what he's said. He certainly doesn't laugh.

I try again.

"You should turn it off," I say. "Save your batteries. We don't know how long we're going to be here."

He swings around to face me, aiming the light in my eyes. There's fear in his voice. "What d'you mean? You said they'd be coming looking for us!"

"They should be. They will be."

"Well, then. As you're always right, these batteries should last okay, shouldn't they?"

"I'm not always right."

He doesn't say anything to that, just swings the beam of light away from me, playing it over the walls once again. The rock looks to me as if it's getting wetter, as if it's sweating with the effort of keeping us trapped.

"How long we been down here, anyway?" he asks.

I look at my diver's watch. I've still got it. Waterproof to one hundred fifty feet.

How do they know? Send a diver down, I suppose.

Whatever, it must be dark that far down. The watch has got luminous hands.

"About an hour," I say.

"That all? It feels like a week."

And the week we've actually been here, Tozer? How long does that feel?

—

We left on Monday, only eleven minutes later than Axelmann's "nine o'clock sharp, without fail."

When Dad drove us through the school gates the bus was already there, waiting, its engine ticking over. It hadn't been cleaned for the occasion. A thin layer of grime covered the back of it. Somebody had scrawled "and don't forget to wash behind your rears" in the muck.

There was a cardboard sign in the back window. FERNEHAM SCHOOL SAFARI. The faces of Greg Yeandle and Flick Harris were looking out above it. They saw me, then turned back again.

Cars were pulling up, unloading parents and students, bags and baggage. Each went their different ways. Bags and baggage went to the bus driver for thumping into the luggage compartment. Parents went to line the sidewalk, to talk to those they'd only nod at in future, laughing and telling each other how much they'd been looking forward to the week.

I went to find a seat on the bus.

Somebody had made a mistake and booked a forty-nine seater. With only twenty of us going, there was plenty of room. I found a seat on my own, not far from the front.

I looked out of the window. Mom gave a little wave, disguising it as a brush of her hair, as if she didn't want to embarrass me. Or herself. Or Dad.

He was next to her, his hands moving as he jabbered at somebody's parents, not noticing that they were more interested in looking at the bus than at him. Once he looked my way and gave a little nod. I didn't know what it was meant to say.

Nobody came to sit next to me.

New arrivals, clattering up the steps and checking to see who's where, would head past and on down the aisle toward where Greg and Flick had set up court in the middle of the wide backseat.

Suddenly the general babble is pierced by a shout.

"Here he comes!"

Tozer's lumbering down the road toward us, a single bulging duffel bag slung over his shoulder. Nobody's come to see him off.

"Quick, spread out!"

As Tozer tramps up the steps and heads down the aisle toward the back of the bus he's met by a volley of excuses.

"Sorry, Tosh, this seat's taken."

"And this one."

"Saving this one for somebody."

Then Greg's clear voice. "That one's free, Tosh."

There's shuffling and grunting as Tozer heaves his stuff up onto the luggage rack and then flops down on the seat he's been awarded. I look around. He's sitting on his own too.

Up at the front I can just see the heads of Mr. Lomax and Mr. Redrow, the other teachers coming with us. They're both youngish, both newish, both unlikely to question Axelmann's authority. The man himself is talking to the bus driver and checking a map.

Then Axelmann stands up. He's at his jolly best as he calls the roll.

"Harris?"

Flick's voice from the back. "Here."

"Afraid you might be. Yeandle?"

"Here."

"Good. At least there'll be somebody who can run a mile without collapsing. Monkey?"

"Here."

"Of course you are. I felt the vibrations when you came aboard. Edwards?"

"Here."

No comment.

Axelmann puts a final tick on his clipboard, looks around, then nods to the driver. There's a burst of engine power, a burst of waving from outside, and then we're around the corner and on the way.

"Right," says Axelmann as we go, "that's the last you'll see of Mommy for a week. I'm your mommy now."

He waits for the laughs and false crying to die down.

"But unlike your mommy, I'm not planning to feed you. We won't be at the Cheddar Gorge until midday, and Combe Warren's another quarter of an hour past that. So as I didn't book a bus with a built-in larder, that means you've got to make whatever grub you've brought with you last the best part of three and a half hours. Right? So don't stuff it all before we've left town."

The hubbub still hasn't died down from the mommy crack, so he has to raise his voice a bit.

"Hear that, did you, Monkey?"

Immediate quiet, waiting for what's to come next. "Don't eat all your bananas at once."

Heads swivel around. Laughing heads, all looking toward Tozer. And what's he doing? He's sitting there grinning, pleased with life.

Can't you see they're laughing at you? Don't you care?

I only turned around once more on the journey.

Tozer was kneeling on his seat, looking over the head-rest toward the Greg and Flick show at the back.

He was still grinning, even though nobody was taking any notice of him.

Axelmann wasn't far out. What with a quick toilet stop on the way, it was 12:15 when he leaned out from his seat and bawled, "Cheddar Gorge!" before going back to whatever he was scribbling on his clipboard.

At first nobody took much notice. But then, as the driver began changing gear to cope with the hill and the bus gradually slowed to a crawl, people began to notice the rock faces towering up on both sides of us. Then even the babblers at the back shut up for a minute.

I found myself looking out on the most amazing sight I'd ever seen in my life.

The rock walls were pitted and rough, although softened somehow by the many ferns and bushes that had managed to seed themselves on the rock face and find enough moisture to grow. But the most incredible thing about it was its height. Even by pressing my cheek against the glass of the bus window, there was no way I could see up to the top of the rock face.

How did it get here?

It was as if we were passing through a gap made by some god from Greek mythology, a god who'd swung an ax and sliced the hill in two. For it was obvious that the gorge hadn't been cut for the road, but the other way around; the road had been laid on a gorge that had been in existence for millions of years.

How high is it?

Since the A-Block episode I'd abandoned my loose-leaf folder and switched to a notebook, the theory being that its pages would stay together should it ever be thrown out of a window. I reached for it now.

By leaning out into the aisle I was able to get a look at the bus's speedometer. Twenty-five miles an hour, up an incline of . . . let's call it two degrees . . . I timed the bus as it ground upward from the bottom of the gorge. Five minutes. A few notebook calculations.

That means . . . more than four hundred feet high. No, four hundred feet deep. Some ax!

I was still thinking about the sight when, fifteen minutes later, the bus scrunched to a halt at the end of a narrow gravel track.

As it does so, the babbling reaches a crescendo. All around me they're leaping up and grabbing bags. Until, that is, Axelmann gets to his feet and plants himself at the head of the aisle.

"Sit down, sit down. Nobody's going anywhere yet."

A frustrated hush as the clipboard comes out again.

"Welcome to Combe Warren," says Axelmann. "Now, while you lot have been enjoying yourselves, some of us have been making plans."

He points a finger out of the window on my side. "Kindly look thataway."

I look. Those on the other side of the bus crowd into the aisle.

We all find ourselves gazing at a row of squat, flat-roofed wooden cabins. They're lined up along one side of a large square, spaced apart and shaded by trees. On the other side of the square there's a couple of smaller huts, plus one that's much larger.

This one's got wire over its windows and a flight of steps leading up to a veranda. It looks like something out of an old film. I imagine Axelmann, dressed in a cowboy outfit, sitting on a rocking chair, smoking a pipe and strumming a guitar.

Well, he's certainly singing the same old song.

"Are you listening, Monkey? See those cabins? You'll be sleeping in one of them, not up in one of the trees. Got that?"

The laughter rises, then fades.

"Right. I'll be in cabin one, along with Mr. Lomax and Mr. Redrow. The rest of you will be sharing cabins two to six."

The clipboard comes up.

"Listen for your name, and you'll find out which one. We'll be running a competition for best cabin, with a prize at the end of the week. Anybody who has to ask me afterward what number cabin he's in will find his squad starting with fifty penalty points straight away. Right, cabin two. Why don't we call you *Eagle* squad . . ."

Sharing?

That's when it sank in.

Don't ask me why, but until that moment it simply hadn't occurred to me that I wouldn't be in a room on my own.

My mind's spinning as Axelmann goes through the lists on his clipboard.

"Cabin three, *Kestrel* . . . Cabin four, *Hawk*."

Sharing a room. Not on my own. "It'll do you good, Daniel . . ."

"Cabin five, let's call you—*Falcon*. . . ."

By the time he gets to the end I know what's coming. I feel that familiar cold hand tightening its grip but tighter than it's ever done before.

"Last, and probably least—cabin six."

Axelmann looks toward the backseat.

"Leader—Greg Yeandle. You're responsible for what goes on in your cabin, Yeandle. Got that? Any trouble, and I'll set Monkey on you."

Overplayed groaning from the back.

"Yes, you're in cabin six as well, Monkey. It's easy to find. Go to number five, and number six is right next door."

Axelmann quickly glances down at his clipboard. He doesn't have to. I can tell him.

"Harris. Cabin six for you too. And, finally, to bring the squad's IQ average up to something approaching normal . . ."

I look up at him.

"Edwards. Cabin six. Cube root of 216 if plain old number six is too simple for you."

He doesn't look at me.

"What are we called, sir?" It's Yeandle, taking the lead already.

"Well now . . ." Axelmann chews slowly. "As all the other squads have been named after birds of prey, why don't we call you—*Vulture* squad?"

Laughter.

"Because they're a dead loss," yells somebody.

Yeandle shouts, "You mean, because we'll be eating the rest of you for breakfast. You'll all be dead meat!"

There's more laughter, but it didn't sound to me as though he was joking.

"Well, let's wait and see who eats who for breakfast," says Axelmann.

And this time he *is* looking at me.

———

Dead meat.

Greg Yeandle's words flit into my mind as, in the beam of Tozer's flashlight, a drop of water falls from somewhere above us to the floor of our pit.

Hesitantly, he turns the light downward, searching for where it's just landed with a gentle plop.

A couple of small puddles have formed. One of them is spreading toward the knapsack on the ground. Tozer turns the light away then, as if he hasn't got the strength to resist, aims it back to the spot again.

"Is it waterproof?" he asks. His voice is shaking.

"What?"

"That knapsack."

"I don't know. Does it make a difference?"

"There might be something in it. If it gets ruined, we'll get the blame. I don't want to get the blame. It wasn't my fault."

The beam of light wanders back and forth as he babbles on.

"It wasn't my fault. We were sent in here, weren't we? Told to come in here, weren't we?"

"Sure," I say.

I remember the words I'd heard just before it happened.

"Watch out. It's slippery in here."

And I look down at the body on the ground in front of us.

I look at his head, propped up on his knapsack as best we could manage. In Tozer's beam of light I see his hair, usually so carefully combed, now matted with blood.

And I can't get Yeandle's phrase out of my mind.

Dead meat.

Chapter 6

"What a dump!"

Greg Yeandle flung his bags down on the nearest bed, before stalking into the center of the cabin and shuffling himself around in a slow circle as he examined the place. Flick followed suit, then Tozer. I stood by the door.

The cabin was an oblong, perhaps twenty feet by fifteen. Wooden floor, wooden walls, wooden ceiling, wooden everything including four narrow wooden beds, each with a chunky wooden cabinet beside it.

Two of the beds were tucked nicely alongside one of the long walls. Between them, fixed to the wall, a flat heater was squeaking out some warmth.

The third bed was at the far end of the cabin. It was jammed alongside a small white sink. One of its faucets was dripping gently.

Above the sink hung a small mirror. Flick briefly checked his hair in it, then said, "Who's going where, then?"

Greg had tossed his bags onto bed number four, just inside the door and perfectly placed for every incoming draft.

As Flick asks his question, Yeandle picks up his bags again and carries them over to one of the beds next to the heater.

"This one will do for me."

Flick shoves his case across the floor with his foot, then flings himself face first onto the other bed on that side of the room.

"Hard or what?" he yells, thumping the pillow with his fist. He doesn't move, though.

Greg points to the third bed, up by the sink.

"There y'are, Tosh. You can have that one."

Tozer looks that way, then back again. "Why?"

Greg squares his shoulders and puts on a sergeant-major voice. "Because your leader says so, soldier!"

Just like Axelmann. "Because I say so."

Flick pops his head up, like a tortoise. "Prime position, Tosh. Next to the sink. You can wash your smelly feet without getting out of bed."

By the door, a fire extinguisher is mounted on the wall. Greg lifts it off and holds it at his hip like a red machine gun.

"And no smoking in bed either, Tosher. Or Danny'll put you out." Smile, no teeth, as he winks at me. "Won't you, Danny-boy?"

Friendly. Charming. But the message is clear. The fire extinguisher is nearest your bed, the fourth bed, the worst bed, draftland, chilly corner. Your bed, and don't let's have any arguments about it.

I lay my case flat on the bed and start unzipping it.

That's when Tozer asks, "Why can't I have the bed Flick's on? Why can't I be near the heater?"

He hasn't moved, hasn't shifted his duffel bag from his shoulder.

For a moment, Greg doesn't know how to handle it. He tries joking.

"Near the heater? You, Tosh? I thought you were the tough one. Right, Flick?"

"Man of Iron," said Flick. "Impervious to all known forces."

"Strong, hard, impenetrable . . ."

"Thick."

I see just the faintest flicker of anger cross Tozer's face. Greg spots it too. He holds his hands up.

"Okay, okay. Never let it be said I'm not a fair-minded leader. I'll tell you what. We'll draw for it."

Flick's not so happy himself now. "What? How? Flip a coin?"

"No," said Greg, thinking. "I've got it." He looks at the other two.

Get the message, Danny-boy? You're not included. You're staying where you are, come what may.

"Spuds up," says Greg.

"What?" says Flick.

"Spuds. One potato, two potato. Remember? The way we always used to pick sides for games."

"When we were kids," says Flick. He's annoyed now, a right-hand man being given less than his due. "If we've got to do this, what's wrong with flipping a coin?"

"Because you could have one of your double-headed quarters for all Tosh knows, couldn't you?" says Greg. "This way, nobody knows who's going to win." His voice rises as he poses the question: "Do they?"

Suddenly, Flick falls in. He nods, as if convinced by Greg's argument. "Fair enough. Suppose not."

"All right, Tosher?"

Tozer looks as if he's been asked the sixty-four-thousand-dollar question.

He doesn't know. The other pair do, but he doesn't. Probably never has.

Tozer nods, too, then. "Right."

"Good. That's agreed. Last one in gets the bed. Come on, hold 'em up."

As Tozer and Flick hold out their fists, Greg moves around so that he's facing them. Tozer is on his left, Flick to his right. As soon as I see this, I know who he's going to start with—and who is going to win.

"One potato . . ." He taps Tozer's right fist.

"Two potato . . ." He taps Tozer's left fist.

"Three potato . . ." Now Greg taps Flick's right fist.

"Four . . ." Flick's left fist.

Then back to the start. "Five potato, six potato, seven potato, *more!*"

As he says the last word he knocks at Flick's left fist

with his own. Looking pleased, Tozer watches as Flick hooks his fist behind his back.

"Good start, Tosher," says Greg. "Looks like you could be the winner here."

He begins counting again.

"One potato, two potato . . ." tapping Tozer's right fist, then his left.

"Three potato, four . . ." Flick's right fist then, with his left missing, on to Tozer's right again.

"Five potato, six potato, seven potato, *more*!" He thumps down on Tozer's left fist with a flourish.

"Even Steven," he says. "Exciting stuff, eh? Who will be the winner?"

It's obvious that, of the three of them, Tozer's the only one who doesn't know the answer. Greg starts the count for the final time.

"One potato, two potato . . ." Flick's remaining fist, then Tozer's.

"Three potato, four . . ." And again.

"Five potato, six potato, seven potato, *more*!"

As Tozer's right fist is knocked down—and Flick looks suitably surprised—Greg shakes his head. "Harris the winner. Bad luck, Tosh."

What should I say? It's a fix? If you've worked it out, you can make whoever you want become the winner because the order never changes?

What's the point? Why get on the wrong side of Yeandle and Harris? They're Tozer's friends, not mine. If he's dumb enough to be taken in by them, why should I worry?

I turned back to my unpacking. As I did, I caught a glimpse of Axelmann. He'd been watching through the cabin window. Moments later he was opening the door.

"All sorted out, Yeandle?"

"Yes, sir. Just deciding beds, weren't we, men?"

"So I noticed," says Axelmann. "Spuds turn out Monkey's way, did they?"

"Not quite," says Greg. "Luck of the draw, you know?"

Axelmann looks across at Tozer. Slow head shake. *Yes, he knows.*

"Monkey and Brains in the same squad," he says to Yeandle. "I may just have given you too big a handicap."

Yeandle looks as if he'd like to agree with him, plead for a change, but doesn't.

"Free time now," Axelmann snaps suddenly. "Dinner at six-thirty sharp."

He slams the door shut behind him as he leaves.

I finish my unpacking without a word, then go outside myself.

Behind me, Greg and Flick are looking in the mirror and laughing as they compare hairstyles.

Tozer is lying on his bed, staring silently at the ceiling.

—

"Is he dead yet?" asks Tozer.

I bend down, feel once again for the carotid

artery at the side of his neck. The pulse is still strong.

"No," I say.

"He hasn't moved, has he?" says Tozer. "Not since it happened."

It's not a question, more a statement of what we both know.

Then, as if he's just worked it out, "He must have hit his head as we came down. I know I didn't land on him. He can't say I landed on him. Did you land on him?"

"No." I point at the lumps of rock scattered about the floor. "It could have been one of those. Anything."

"Has he lost much blood, d'you reckon? It's bad if you lose a lot of blood, ain't it?"

"Yes. But I don't think he's lost that much."

As I say it, I try to dab away a little of the blood from the matted hair. Tozer gets to his feet, shines the light down, but doesn't bend to join me.

Suddenly he says angrily, "Why you doing that? Been no friend of yours this week, has he?"

Who has been a friend of mine this week, Tozer? You?

No. Only one person—and I haven't been sure about him half the time . . .

—

There was a narrow pathway leading away from the cabins. It was soft and springy with wood chippings. I followed it, away from the voices and sudden shouts, through the trees.

As I walked, I thought.

That tree—what diameter is it? How tall? What volume of wood? How many matchsticks would it make?

And then the trees and sounds were behind me, and I was walking in the clear, down toward a rickety jetty at the edge of a lake. For the second time that day, I found myself staring at scenery I'd never known existed.

Curving around the far side of the lake, walls of the same sort of green-clad rock I'd seen in the Cheddar Gorge rose high out of the water. It looked as if the god who'd carved open the gorge had put down his ax when he got here and scooped out the earth with his hand instead.

No—it looked as if this place *was* the god's hand, with the rock walls his fingers, the water trapped in his palm.

How? How did it get here? How did it come about?

Caught up in it all, I didn't hear the stranger whistling until he stopped, close behind me.

"Lost?" he asks.

I spin around, shake my head. "No."

He smiles. "Just lost in thought, eh?"

I wait for an Axelmann-style wisecrack, but it doesn't come. He just turns away and gazes out across the lake himself.

Without looking at me, he says, "What do you reckon, then?"

"Sorry."

A wave of his hand, still not looking at me. "All this. What do you think of it?"

I look at him, side-on. He's not tall, not big. But he looks as solid as one of the trees back there. His face is weather-beaten, as if he's spent all his life outdoors. He's wearing an old sweater, frayed at the cuffs, check shirt peeping out of the collar.

"It's . . ."

He doesn't take his hands out of his pockets, doesn't turn, just tilts his head slightly in my direction.

"Different?"

It just slips out. "Amazing."

I see his eyebrows flick up in surprise. Now he turns so that he's looking straight at me. "Amazing? In what way?"

I'm struggling for the right words. For some reason, I desperately want to find them.

"It's . . . I don't know . . . the rocks, I think." I'm pointing out across the lake. "Like on the way here, in the Cheddar Gorge . . ."

He's nodding, smiling, encouraging me to say what I feel without actually saying anything himself.

"The strength it must have taken to do it. I can't imagine it. I wouldn't know how to start calculating it. But . . . I can feel it . . ."

Suddenly I'm turning my back on him. I don't know him from Adam, I can't explain what I've just said, and I'm waiting for him to start laughing.

But he doesn't. He simply says, "What's your name?"

"Daniel. Daniel Edwards."

"You know, Daniel, I think you're right. I can feel it, too, whatever it is. Always have."

As he strolls off, he starts whistling again. He's still got his hands in his pockets. He looks like the most contented person I've ever seen in my life. I wonder who he is, and where he found his happiness.

I watched him go then headed back through the trees, back toward the noise and clatter.

Back to my first clash with Tozer.

Chapter 7

We ate dinner in the large hut, seated at a long table. Axelmann sat at the head, with Mr. Lomax and Mr. Redrow on either side of him.

No sooner had we finished eating than Axelmann is getting them to help him move the table and is yelling at us to move our chairs to the sides.

"Arrange yourselves in a circle!"

As soon as we've done it, he steps into the center.

"Teamwork," he says, "this week is all about teamwork. Working together."

He turns slowly in a circle of his own as he goes on, "And the first thing we are going to learn about working together is trust. Got that? Trust."

"Cluck-cluck-cluck."

Axelmann whirls around toward the source of the chicken impersonation, then sees who's responsible.

"Thank you, Yeandle. I haven't heard that one since this time last year. No, not trussed, as in trussed up like a chicken, but trust—as in relying on each other. Putting yourself in the hands of another person."

"Oooh," coos Flick Harris. "Nice."

The laughter rises to a peak. It's the sign for Axelmann to play his usual trick.

"Monkey. Come here."

He beckons Tozer into the center of the circle. The group immediately quiets down, not wanting to miss any of the fun they're now expecting.

Tozer steps forward and stands in front of Axelmann. Close together, I can see that, young as he is, Tozer's almost as tall as him.

"Turn around," says Axelmann to Tozer. "Face the window."

Tozer does as he's told, grinning at the people in front of him.

"Right then, Monkey," says Axelmann. He's talking to the back of Tozer's head. "Now, nice and loud. Do you trust me?"

Tozer begins to turn around to look at him.

"I didn't say you could look at me!" shouts Axelmann.

Tozer snaps back into position.

"Monkey, do you trust me?" Axelmann asks again.

"Er—yes, sir."

"Sure?"

Half happy, half anxious. "Yes, sir."

"Good." Axelmann's cool and serious now. "So in that case you'll do exactly what I tell you to do. Agreed?"

Tozer nods.

"Right, then. Put your arms out from your sides. I want you to imagine you're a plank."

The suggestion gets its intended response. There's a burst of laughter as Flick says in a stage whisper, "Shouldn't be hard. He's as thick as one."

"What I mean is keep as stiff as a board, Monkey," says Axelmann. "Can you do that?" As Tozer nods again, he says, "Right. Now fall backward."

"Sir?"

"You said you trusted me, Monkey. Well, prove it. Fall backward. I'm going to catch you."

In spite of himself, Tozer looks around. He sees that Axelmann's taken a couple of steps back from where he was. He's going to have to fall halfway to the floor before he's caught.

Slowly, he faces forward again. He extends his arms, looking like a frightened scarecrow.

"Right, fall!" snaps Axelmann.

Tozer hesitates.

"Fall!"

Closing his eyes, Tozer falls . . . then jerks a leg out to save himself before he gets anywhere near Axelmann's arms. He ends up staggering back into his chest instead.

"Useless," growls Axelmann as Tozer levers himself away. "Do it again."

Tozer returns to his position.

"Don't move your heels this time, Monkey. Imagine they're nailed to the floor. Got that?"

"Yes, sir."

"Now—you said you trusted me. So, come on. Fall!"

Tozer tries again. But again he puts a foot back to save himself.

"Come on, Monkey, we're only here for a week," says Axelmann. He's getting irritated now. "Once more."

Yet again Tozer does the same thing. This time he ends up thumping Axelmann's shoulder with his head.

Axelmann gives up. He looks at Tozer as though he's something he's just found on the sole of his shoe. "Monkey, you're a waste of time. Back to your place."

"Right," he says to the rest of us, "you get the idea? Pair up with somebody in your squad. Let's see if you can do better."

"Looks like me and you, Gregso," says Flick immediately.

Greg looks my way. "Which leaves you with Tosher, Danny-boy. And the best of luck."

As I meet up with Tozer, Axelmann comes our way.

"Well, well. The terrible twosome. Maybe you'll be able to trust Brains here more than you could me, Monkey. Brains, you're the catcher."

Around us others are trying the exercise. Axelmann looks across as Flick falls back perfectly into Greg Yeandle's arms.

"Good," says Axelmann.

He turns to us. Tozer hasn't moved. "Well, what are you waiting for?"

"He'll drop me."

"Oh, ye of little faith," sighs Axelmann. "He won't drop you—will you, Edwards?"

"No," I say. And I mean it. Tozer's a lot taller and heavier than me, but I've got it worked out.

Tozer gives me a look. "You'd better not. You'd just better not."

"Come on, then," says Axelmann, chewing cheerfully.

Slowly, Tozer turns his back on me. I step behind him. I'm planning to stand closer than I should. It's simple math, center of gravity. If he doesn't fall too far, his feet will take most of his weight, not my arms. And if I hold them out stiff in front of me, I reckon I'll be able to cope.

Fat chance.

"Back," says Axelmann when he sees where I'm standing.

"What?"

"You heard. Back. Another two paces."

"I won't be able to hold him."

"Of course you will. Trust me."

He knows what he's doing. He's put me just far enough to make all the difference. Now he stands in front of Tozer.

"This time you *are* going to do it right, Monkey," he says quietly. "Now—arms out."

Axelmann moves to Tozer's side. Then he thrusts his jogging-suited leg forward so that his foot is jammed up tight against Tozer's heels. There's no way he can put a foot back to save himself now.

"Ready . . ." says Axelmann.

I'm inching forward, hoping against hope that Axelmann won't spot me. Unless I can get closer, I know I'm not going to be able to hold him.

"Steady . . ."

It's at that moment, when neither of us is ready, that Axelmann loops a hand around and shoves Tozer hard in the chest.

Before I can brace myself he's falling backward. His arms start flailing in panic. They're still whirling as he falls back and thumps into me. For a second I think I've got him. But Axelmann's shove has made just that bit of difference. He's too much.

My arms give way and then my legs. Before I know it he's hit the floor with a wallop and dragged me down on top of him.

"Weirdo!"

That's all Tozer yells. Just that. But it silences the others. All around us they're turning to see what's happened, gathering around us in a circle, looking down on us like we're a football in the middle of a pileup.

I look up at the faces. They're all laughing—all except Axelmann's.

"You seem to have let Monkey down, Brains," he

says as Tozer angrily shoves me aside and scrambles to his feet. "I don't think he's going to trust you much from now on."

Through my mind flashes just one thought.

And I'm not going to trust you, Axelmann.

—

"There must be a ledge up there."

In the blackness I say it idly, almost to myself, as the thought occurs to me.

Water trickles down walls. It doesn't drip. For water to drip, there has to be something overhanging for it to drip from.

Tozer swings his light upward instantly.

"Where?"

"Where the drips are coming from."

"Well, where the hell's that!" he shouts, waving his light about madly.

It's no good. The beam's not strong enough. The sliver of light far above is no help at all either.

I get my own flashlight out for a moment and flick it on. It flares brightly but still not enough to cut through the blackness above us.

"It's too dark to tell. It must be on the other side of where we came in. High up."

"It might not be high up," says Tozer. His voice rises with hope. "It might be a little bit up. One of us might be able to reach it. Get up there. It could be a way out. I could go. I'm a faster runner than you. I could get help. Come back for you." He motions toward the figure on the ground. "And him."

"If we can't see the ledge then it's too high to reach," I say flatly.

"How do you know!"

"Look!" I shout.

I aim my light up again. It illuminates six feet above our heads, no more, before being eaten by the blackness.

I turn it off then. All we're left with now is the tired glow of Tozer's flashlight.

"Turn yours off as well," I say. "The batteries are going."

"Get stuffed."

Big, brave Tozer.

"Turn it off," I say.

He turns the fading beam back to the floor, to the closed eyes down there.

"I don't feel like it."

As I look at him an anger starts rising from somewhere within me, an anger the like of which I've never known before.

He's cheating me.

Tozer the Tough.

Tozer the Fearless.

Here I am, wanting him to be tough for the first time in my life, wanting him to show me he's fearless, show me he's not scared.

But he isn't fearless. He is scared.

He's cheating me.

"Turn it off!" I scream.

Startled by the voice that even I don't recognize, Tozer jerks the light up from the floor to look at me. His mouth opens, as if he's going to say something.

He doesn't. Without a word, he clicks off his flashlight.

The inky blackness clamps down on us again, like a blindfold.

Like a blindfold . . . and the lesson Tozer taught me.

Chapter 8

That was on Tuesday morning.

After breakfast and some free time, we'd gathered in the large hut again to find the long table cleared and relaid, not with plates and cutlery but with equipment. The stranger was there, too, the man I'd met by the lake. Axelmann introduced him.

"Gentlemen," he says grandly, as if he thinks we're special, "let me introduce Mr. John Matthews."

The stranger gazes around the hut, his eyes seeming to take us all in at once. "Call me Lonnie," he says quietly.

"Mr. John Matthews," repeats Axelmann, tight-lipped, "who, for reasons best known to himself, likes to be called Lonnie."

"It was what my mom called me."

A small ripple of laughter goes around the table. Axelmann smiles now, but it's only on his face for an instant.

"Mr. Matthews—Lonnie—is the warden here. Has

been since I don't know when. Since Noah tested his ark on the lake probably. That right, Lonnie?"

If Axelmann's trying to score a point, it doesn't work. Lonnie simply nods in agreement.

"Twenty-three years."

"And if you want to know what a warden does, then the answer's everything. Guide, equipment fixer . . . head cook and bottle washer. So if you want any bottles washed or heads cooked, Lonnie's your man."

More laughter, this time for Axelmann. He looks happier.

"Anything goes wrong," he adds, "Lonnie here will sort things out. Just make sure nothing does go wrong, though. Got that, you lot?"

He looks down on us for a couple of seconds. Nobody knows whether he's trying to impress us or Lonnie. One or two mutter a "yes, sir."

I look at the two men. One, Axelmann, trying to be casual and commanding. The other, Lonnie, looking it without trying at all.

He gestures to the long table, laden with equipment. "All ready for you, Mr. Axelmann."

Axelmann gives him a curt nod, then turns to us.

"Right, you lot," he barks. "Get yourselves one of everything. Especially a backpack," he shouts as the stampede begins. "That's what it's all got to go in."

He sits down in a corner while Lomax and Redrow scurry about trying to sort things out. It's like the

January sales. I manage to find a decent backpack, with two side pockets, its blue canvas hardly worn. Then a compass, a map, a whistle, a flashlight.

Mr. Lomax drops a cellophane-wrapped packed lunch into my arms. Mr. Redrow, in charge of drinks, slides a small squashy carton of orange juice toward me, the sort that demonstrates the principle of the siphon if you're not careful and squirts the stuff all over you when you stop sucking at the straw.

One section of the table is laden with boots and waterproof gear. Lonnie is helping out there. He asks my shoe size, then hands over a pair of hiking boots. A clean, woolly sock is tucked inside each.

Next a wet-weather suit, waterproof jacket and pants.

"Don't put it on, Monkey," yells Axelmann as Tozer starts hauling on his jacket. It's bright orange and huge. "Socks and boots on. Pack the rest."

I find a quiet corner and lay my things out.

Lonnie, boots all issued, begins wandering around. He says something to Greg Yeandle, who shrugs and pulls a face as Lonnie moves away. Before I realize it, he's kneeling down beside me.

"If I was you, Daniel," he says quietly as I start shoving things into my backpack, "I'd pack all that in a different order."

The fact that he's remembered my name passes me by. I ask, "Why? What difference does it make?"

It's the sort of question that would have made Axel-mann go purple.

I wait for "Because I say so . . ."

It doesn't come. Instead he says, "Because it would make life easier for you."

"How?"

Am I testing him? I don't know. But, if I am, he passes.

"By making sure the things you need most are close at hand. And so that you know exactly where they are in an emergency."

Simple question, simple answer.

He pats the pockets on either side of my backpack. "Left for food, right for life," he says.

As he watches, I put my packed lunch and a bar of chocolate I've been saving into the left pocket. Into the right goes the map and compass. Also the whistle we've been told to blow if we ever lose contact with the others.

"And the flashlight," says Lonnie.

"Why?"

"That can save your life, too, you know." He looks around the floor at the rest of my stuff. "As for every-thing else—LIFO is the thing to remember."

I look at him. "LIFO? Is that an acronym?"

There's the hint of a smile. "Yes, it is. It stands for Last In, First Out. In other words, pack last the things you'll need first."

"Like what?"

He looks around—and picks up my notebook. It's perched on top of my waterproof gear, waiting to be packed.

"What about this?" says Lonnie.

I panic, reach out for it.

"It's nothing. It's mine," I say quickly.

Lonnie just nods. Doesn't try to open it or look in it. He just hands it to me straight away. He's noticed the well-thumbed state of it, though.

"Use it a lot, do you?" he asks.

Relieved, I mumble, "Yes. A lot."

"Then it's worth packing at the top, I'd say. Wouldn't you?"

We spent the morning walking. I almost enjoyed it.

As Axelmann stomped ahead like some pioneering explorer, with Yeandle and company tagging along close behind, I was left pretty much alone. I amused myself by tracking our route, taking regular compass bearings from a direction beacon I could see in the distance.

Then we stopped for lunch. We'd been following a track across open ground. Now, as the track began to skirt a heavily wooded area, Axelmann called a halt.

Flick Harris tottered theatrically off the track and collapsed onto the apron of grass in front of the trees. Greg Yeandle joined him, groaning loudly about the state of his feet. Tozer copied them.

"Watch it," said Axelmann. "You might just have something to groan about in a minute." He shouted to the trees. "Lunchtime!"

Over on the far side, Yeandle and company were unloading their backpacks to pull out squashed drink cartons and flattened cellophane packages.

Left for food, right for life.

I put my map and compass away and dug out my uncrushed lunch.

When we'd finished, Axelmann stood up. Whatever else he'd eaten, his meal had finished with a fresh stick of chewing gum. His jaw was working overtime.

"Right, then. Time for exercise number two."

From somewhere he'd conjured up a handful of black cloth strips. As we stayed down on the grass he strolled among us, tossing them to different people.

One landed in my lap.

"Take your partners!" he yells, as though he's announcing a dance. A look down at me, then across to where Tozer is still sprawled on his back.

"Monkey!" he yells. "Over here!"

Tozer lumbers slowly to his feet, then starts moving toward us. "Come on," yells Axelmann. "Chop, chop!" Tozer looks like I feel.

"Why me?" I ask Axelmann. "Why me and him?"

Axelmann stares at me. "Because you're made for each other," he says.

He begins shouting orders to the world.

"Back onto the track. Face away from the trees

toward the open ground. Right, those of you who've been given blindfolds—put them on your partners."

Tozer doesn't say a word as I reach up and wind the black strip of cloth over his eyes, then tie it into a knot at the back of his head.

Axelmann marches up and down, examining the blindfolds like the commander of a firing squad.

"This exercise," he shouts when everything's to his satisfaction, "is also about trust. Those of you with blindfolds on have got to do exactly what your partner tells you. Without fail. Trust him completely. Clear?"

I hear odd calls of "yes, sir."

Tozer says nothing.

Axelmann moves our way.

"Is that clear, Monkey?" he chews. "I know it'll be hard after yesterday, but you've got to trust Brains here. Okay?"

"Yes, sir."

Another world proclamation. "Those of you without blindfolds, you've got to guide your partner forward. Give him nice clear instructions. Understand?"

There doesn't seem anything to understand. Stretching out in front of us is the open ground on the other side of the track.

Forward, forward, forward. What's the problem?

I should have known better.

"Right, guides. Turn your partners around."

I look at Axelmann. "You've got it, Brains," he says. "So that he's facing the trees."

Slowly, I turn Tozer around. Axelmann steps behind me and turns him back a touch.

"Guides, your job is to get your partner safely through those trees. Through them, okay? Not around them. No following the footpath for a mile, no directions back to the bus. Through them. Now, when you're ready—go!"

He looks at me, then at Tozer. Chew. Grin. "And may God be with you, Monkey," he adds.

Is it a coincidence? Maybe everybody else is in the same sort of position. But as I look ahead I see that Axelmann's maneuvered Tozer so that he's directly in front of just about the biggest, most awkward tree of the lot. It's got thick low-hanging branches sweeping away on either side of its trunk. Beneath it there's a layer of dead leaves covering the ground. Broken branches are peeping out from them like crocodiles lying in wait.

"Where am I going then?" asks Tozer, finally.

"Forward," I say.

Tozer begins to inch slowly toward the trees.

"Keep going forward. Keep going."

The tree is getting closer with every step he takes, its branches looking bigger and more awkward. And in front of it there's a thin sapling I hadn't noticed.

Come on, think, think. It's a problem to be solved. Think.

Suddenly, I see the answer. It's all a matter of measurements and angles, a three-dimensional puzzle.

"Left by twenty degrees," I say. That should get him past the sapling.

"What?"

"Bear left by twenty degrees."

Tozer turns himself to the left. But not by enough.

"More. Another ten degrees." He turns farther to his left, but still not by enough.

Before I can give him another instruction, a whippy branch from the sapling catches him high up on the shoulder, then bounces up to slap him hard on the face. He swears.

"You didn't turn enough. Go another ten degrees to your left."

Tozer starts swinging himself that way. As he gets to the point I want, I cheat and stop him with my hand before he can turn too far.

"No holding, Edwards!" bellows Axelmann. "Verbal instructions only!"

"Forward," I say.

Tozer moves off again. He's got his arms held up in front of his face, now.

"You're going to have to stop in fifteen feet or so," I say. Tozer slows to a shuffle as I continue, "Forward, forward . . . stop."

I've led him to one side of the massive tree trunk. A thick branch is in front of him at knee height. Another, not so thick but thick enough, is about level with his chest. If he hits either of those branches he's going to feel it.

"Listen," I say. "There are two branches in front of you. To get under the top one you've got to duck your head by about a foot. The bottom one's about two feet off the ground. All right?"

Tozer says nothing, just stretches out his arms like a sleepwalker to feel what's in front of him. Axelmann's over like a shot.

"And no feeling your way!" he yells. "Guide's instructions only."

He inspects Tozer's predicament with relish. "Go on then, Monkey. Do what he's told you to do."

"Duck down by about a foot. Foot up two feet," I repeat.

Tozer bends down—but not enough. Edging forward, he lifts his foot—but not enough. His foot catches on the lower branch and he tips forward, clouting his head on the top branch.

Axelmann looks on, loving it. As Tozer lands on his face in the dead leaves he turns away.

"Change over!"

Tozer's ripped the blindfold off before the echo's died away. He gets to his feet and holds it out, balancing it on his fingertips.

"Your go, Weirdo. Turn around."

Stepping behind me, he ties the blindfold tightly around my eyes. I can feel the knot digging into the back of my head. He grabs hold of my shoulders and shoves me forward. Then he turns me around to face the way I've come.

It's no problem picturing what's in front of me.

The sapling, then the tree I tried to guide him through. It's in front of me. He's brought me back to the same place he started from.

Tozer's fingers dig into my shoulders as he spins me around. Half a turn. And again. Then another half turn.

I'm facing him. I can almost feel his eyes boring through the blindfold.

One more half turn.

I'm facing the way I'd started. I'm facing the way I led him. He's going to get his own back.

"Ready, Weirdo?"

Tozer's voice, from directly behind me. With the blindfold on, I can only imagine the look on his face. It makes him sound even more threatening than usual.

"What happened was your fault," I say. "I told you what to do . . ."

"Told me? You told me *nothing*, Weirdo. Now, it's your turn." He starts to tell me what I've already worked out for myself.

"There's a tree in front of you, a big one. Big, hard branches all over the place, you know? The sort that really hurt when you smack your head on them. You're going straight through that tree, Weirdo."

His hands leave my shoulders. I wait.

"Right, walk forward. Slow, like."

I start forward, bracing myself for the crunch I'm sure is going to come. But, instead, I hear Tozer's voice again.

"Go to ten o'clock."

The surprise stops me. "What?"

"Ten o'clock!" he shouts in my ear. "Tell the time, can't you, Weirdo? Twelve o'clock's straight on. I'm telling you to head for ten o'clock."

I swing to my left. A few more slow paces forward, still tensed, waiting to hit something.

"Eleven o'clock."

I swing halfway back again.

"Forward, forward."

One step. Then another. The sapling must be close. He's leading me straight into it. I stop, scared.

"Forward!"

As I move off again, I feel a whippy branch brush my head. It's the sapling, it must be. The branch that hit Tozer in the face. He's guided me past it.

Twelve o'clock . . . ten o'clock . . . eleven o'clock.

All my jabbering about angles and degrees had meant nothing to Tozer. It wasn't that I'd given him bad instructions—he just hadn't understood them. I'd been talking my way and it had meant nothing to him.

And now here he is, the school clown, talking his way—and I can understand him. Why? Because he isn't talking a weirdo language, that's why. He's talking a language anyone can understand.

I'm still walking forward.

"Stop!"

I'm in front of the big tree, with its thick branches. Not in the same position he was in, I don't think. The branches may be higher. Or lower.

"Three o'clock."

I swing around to my right.

Now I'm parallel to the branches. How high are they? How low?

"Keep your legs straight. Put your hands on your knees."

I do as I'm told, without thinking, without realizing he's asking me to bend over.

"Right," I hear Tozer say. "Now your head's low enough to go under that top branch."

One instruction. No feet, half feet, fractions of a foot.

"Don't move your head. Lift your left leg." As my foot comes up, "That's far enough. Swing it to your left. And . . . down."

I'm straddling the branch.

"Now your right leg. Lift . . . enough. Across."

I'm over it. But the higher branch must be straight above my head. If he makes me stand up straight . . .

"Hands on knees still. Now, step sideways till I tell you to stop. One, two, three, four. Stop. Stand up."

Slowly, slowly, I ease myself up straight, waiting for the crack on the head.

It doesn't come. I'm through. Tozer's done it. He's got me through.

"Back to twelve o'clock."

"What? Why?"

Tozer's voice, as hard as ever. "The lesson ain't over yet, Weirdo. Back to twelve o'clock."

I turn to my left.

Facing straight ahead again, on into the woods. What's there? I can't remember.

"Forward. One, two, three . . ."

I follow Tozer's instructions as he starts guiding me again. Beneath my feet, the leaves are soft and springy.

"Two o'clock."

On Tozer's command, I swing to my right.

"One o'clock."

Back to my left. Something brushes against my arm. I take another step and get the same sensation on my other side. Branches—branches of two trees. He could have led me straight into either if he'd wanted, but he's guided me between them.

"Back to eleven o'clock. One, two, three . . ."

I go on, obeying Tozer's commands. There's a feeling growing in me, and I can't believe it's happening.

I trust him.

He tells me to duck, and I duck. Turn, and I turn. Straighten, and I straighten. His eyes are my eyes.

I trust him.

"Ten o'clock. On you go, Weirdo. One, two, three, four . . ."

I trust him.

I didn't feel the pain at first.

You know how it is when you pick up something

without realizing it's hot—how your brain takes a few seconds to adjust? That's how it was.

Then, suddenly, the pain breaks through and it's as if I'm surrounded by a thousand claws. They're tearing through my clothes, digging into my skin. I try to turn around, but they're behind me as well now, blocking my way out, ripping at me wherever I try to move. I thrash out with my arms, but it's no good. Every movement just makes the pain worse, just sends another wave of unseen claws onto the attack.

I cry out for help.

But Tozer's stopped helping.

I bend my head to my hands. My fingers tug desperately at the blindfold, pulling it down so that I can see again.

And then I do see—see that Tozer's had his revenge. He's guided me carefully, expertly, perfectly, into a head-high clump of vicious brambles.

I trusted you, Tozer.

He's laughing, now. Behind him, they're all laughing.

"There you go, Weirdo," he laughs. "That's how it's done."

I trusted you.

Chapter 9

The rumbling noise came suddenly, the dull sound of rock moving over rock.

"What's that?" says Tozer at once. They're the first words he's spoken since I yelled at him about the flashlight.

I look up, instinctively shielding my head, half expecting a flurry of rocks to land on me. Nothing does.

"The light!" shouts Tozer, even as I see it. "Look!"

High above us, the thin slit in the rock has widened. A shaft of murky light is pushing its way in now, angling its way across from the entrance of the cave to the wall of rock opposite.

"They've come for us!" shouts Tozer.

Immediately he starts yelling for all he's worth. "Help! Down here! We're down here!"

I join in, shouting and shrieking on the whistle until we're making so much noise we can't hear anything else.

"Sssh!"

We stop and listen.

Nothing.

Instead of the human voices we're hoping for, all we hear is the sound of our own breathing in the silence.

"There was somebody there," Tozer moans softly. "I heard them."

"It must have been the rocks moving," I say. "Near where we came in."

Above us the shaft of light is like a melting silver bar, its solid center turning fuzzier and fuzzier as it meets the blackness we're trapped in at the bottom.

The barest amount manages to reach down to us, but it's enough for me to see the outline of Tozer's face as he looks upward.

"You were right," he says. "There is a ledge up there."

High up toward the gloom in the roof there's a shadow, dark against the shaft of light. It's jutting out from the side of the rock like a broken bridge. As we look at it, small drops of water are falling from the end. And, as I predicted, it is way out of reach.

Maybe it's the disappointment of discovering that the noise we heard wasn't the sound of rescuers coming. Maybe it's seeing the ledge. I don't know. But suddenly he swings around on me.

"Mister know-it-all! Never wrong, are you? Always right!"

Right, Tozer. Two can play at that game. I'm feeling gutted as well, you know. And I'm feeling scared. So what's new?

I snap on my flashlight, shine the beam full in his face.

"So? What if I am right? Is that why you're always on at me, Tozer? Is it? Is that why you can't ever leave me alone? Because I get things right?"

The surprise shows on his face. He tries to turn his head away from the light, as if it's a hand slapping him.

"Is it?" I yell again. I aim the flashlight down at the blood-stained figure on the ground. "You. Him. Is that why I'm fair game for everybody! Is it? I want to know!"

Still he doesn't speak. But I feel the anger subsiding, as if the pressure inside me has been released. I turn off my flashlight, plunge us back into the darkness.

"Tell me," I say, quietly this time. "My hiking boots, for instance. Why? Why did you have to do what you did?"

—

I'd escaped from them as soon as we got back from the blindfold exercise, run away from the Yeandle and Harris wisecracking double act.

"I think Danny-boy's got the needle with Tosher for some reason."

"You're right, Greg. He does seem to be in a bit of a prickly mood."

"Probably 'cause Tosher's a thorn in his side . . ."

Dumping my stuff in the cabin, I'd grabbed my towel and swimming trunks and gone down to the quiet of the lakeside.

At the end of the jetty I took off my boots, then the woolen socks, jamming one inside each boot. I dangled my feet in the water, feeling it flow around them.

After a few minutes I ducked into the trees. Out again, trunks on.

Leaving my clothes in a neat pile beside my boots at the end of the jetty, I slip into the water.

It's cold, much colder than the swimming pool, as if the whole lake has been kept in the fridge. I strike out for the middle.

From the jetty the curve of rock that surrounds the lake looks gray and solid, like the sides of Cheddar Gorge. Closer to, I see differently. The rock is creased and broken, as if the Greek god scored it with his fingernails. It's pockmarked, too, with holes of odd sizes and shapes that are seeping water into the lake.

I turn over and float on my back, staring at the sky, feeling at home, at peace, my mind wandering.

Does a drowning man really come up for air three times? If he does, how was it discovered? By somebody sitting at the side of a river, watching and counting as people went under?

"Oy! Weirdo!"

The shout comes from the jetty.

They've got my clothes.

Tozer, still wearing his orange waterproof jacket, is waving my shirt in the air. Flick's doing the same with my pants. Greg is tossing my boots from one hand to the other.

"Weirdo! Oh, Weir-do!"

I see Tozer's mouth open, hear his taunt arrive a fraction later, like thunder after lightning, like the sound of a baseball after you see it hit the bat.

"Hey!" yells Tozer again. "These yours, are they?"

Greg holds my boots high. "Danny-boy! As leader of *Vulture* squad, I've been inspecting your boots. They look a bit muddy to me."

Flick's voice comes out across the water then. "Greg's right, y'know. They look very muddy indeed!"

"Like they need a real good cleanup," shouts Tozer.

"Or a wash," shouts Greg. "What do you reckon, Tosh? Give them a wash, Tosh?"

"A wash?" Tozer looks at Greg, but he's calling out to me. "You got it, Greg!"

I start swimming back to the jetty but, of course, it's no use. I'm no more than halfway there when Yeandle, holding his arm out as if my boot has some sort of contagious disease, lets it fall into the water with a plop.

I don't shout, don't beg, keep the vow I made to myself that day up in the school library as I watched my precious notes spiraling in the wind. That much I've learned about dealing with the likes of Yeandle. Begging is no use, because they'll still go ahead and do whatever they're threatening just to prove they've got the power.

And if you don't beg? So, they do it anyway, because you've annoyed them. But then, in their hearts, they know it's you who's really the winner.

As I look toward the jetty, Greg is handing my other boot to Tozer.

"Nearly clonked a fish with my one," he crows. "Reckon you can do better, Tosh?"

Tozer, grinning Tozer, takes the boot from his master, holds out his arm, and lets it drop into the water. Suddenly, cutting through their hoots of laughter, comes another voice. It's sharp and angry.

"Hey! What do you think you're doing?"

It's Lonnie, hurrying toward the jetty. As the three of them catch sight of him they drop the rest of my stuff and scuttle back through the trees toward the camp. I hear them cackling as they go.

"Managed to save your shirt and pants, anyway," says Lonnie as I reach the jetty.

"Thanks."

"They dropped your boots in."

"I saw them."

Lonnie begins to stalk down the jetty, the fastest I've seen him move. "Hang on. I'll get a net."

"It's okay."

Tozer was standing directly above the jetty's middle prop when he let my boot go. I jackknife under water at that point and head for the bottom. The water's not only cold it's amazingly clear, as if it's come from a faucet. I find one of the boots straight away and come up for air.

The second surprises me. I dive down three times and don't find it, the final time only coming up when my ears start roaring with the effort of holding my breath. Then, as I hold on to the jetty prop gulping down air, I find it bobbing just beneath the jetty itself, hidden in the shade.

"Air pocket," says Lonnie, as I toss the boot up onto the wooden planks then heave myself up after it.

Principle of the ocean liner. It's not the umpteen thousand tons of steel that float, it's all the air trapped inside it.

He pulls out the sock I'd jammed into the boot. Its end is wet, but most of it's as dry as a bone. "Your sock must have trapped enough air in the toe to stop it from sinking."

Weirdo joke. When is a boot like a pair of pants? When it's got an air pocket. Ha-ha.

Lonnie glares toward the trees, although the three of them are long gone. "Know who they were, do you? I'll sort this out with Mr. Axelmann."

I shake my head. "Forget it. It's the price a weirdo has to pay . . ."

He glances at me. "Weirdo? You look pretty normal to me."

"Well, I'm not. I'm different."

Then, just as he did the first time I met him, he turns away to gaze out across the lake.

"Different from them, you mean? How do you know?"

"Does it matter?" I shout. "I just am! I don't do the things they do. I don't *want* to do the things they do. I don't want to be like them!"

At home, that little outburst would have had me grounded for a week. But Lonnie just nods, slowly. Then he throws me by completely changing tack.

"Ever thought about water, Daniel?" he says. He bends down, picks up a pebble, and tosses it into the lake.

I watch the little ripples form and swim away from where the pebbles went in.

Thought about water? Of course I have. Why are ripples always circular? Why not triangular? Or square? Hexagonal?

"What about it?" I say.

"This lake, Daniel. The water you can see. Where do you think it comes from?"

"Rain, I suppose."

"Right. But not the rainfall that lands here. That wouldn't give you a decent pond. No, most of it comes from up there—from Ebbor Down."

He's pointing away across the lake, to the rock walls rising up from it and beyond, toward the direction beacon I'd seen earlier in the day, on the crest of a wide expanse of green and gray.

"The water that lands on Ebbor Down isn't meant to stay there, Daniel. This is where it's meant to be. And so it runs down. Lots of things try to stop it. But it finds a way. Around stones, between rocks, along cracks, through caves and passageways—somehow it finds a way to get here."

Now he turns to look straight at me.

"That water finds its level, Daniel, the same way you've got to. Those three . . ." —he nods toward the gap in the trees—". . . they're just rocks in your way, obstacles you've got to find your way around."

I know he's trying to help. But he's not. He doesn't know me. He doesn't know Tozer.

"Just like that?" I say. "And what if the rocks won't let you go around them?"

There's a piece of rock on the ground at the side of the jetty. I snatch it up, hold the rock out toward him.

"What if the rocks move and come after you? What if they won't let you alone? If they surround you so there's just no way out?"

Turning, I hurl the rock into the lake. A plume of water shoots high. The ripples race away from it, circles chasing circles.

"I tell you what you do then! You do what those ripples are doing. You run away!"

I pick my sodden boots up from the jetty.

"I've got to get back," I say. "See if I can get these dry before tomorrow."

He nods. "Sure."

He doesn't seem annoyed. I've just let rip at him and it's as if I've just wished him a good morning.

As I hurry away he turns back to the water. He's whistling.

—

"So," I say again to Tozer. "Why? Why chuck my boots into the lake? What was the point?"

In the dark I can almost hear him shrug.

"Bit of a laugh," is all he says.

"A bit of a laugh? Is that all it ever is, then? A bit of a laugh?"

"Reckon so. Bit of laugh, bit of a giggle."

"Is that what Greg says?"

"Yeh."

I pause, remembering what happened afterward.

"He wasn't laughing afterward, though, was he?"

Even though I can barely see him in the gloom, I can't help glancing down at the crumpled figure lying on the ground.

No. Nobody was laughing, then. Especially our beloved leader.

Chapter 10

"Hey up," I heard Greg Yeandle say from behind me. "Looks like Axie's got an announcement to make."

"Maybe it's the winner of the swimming boots championship," said Flick.

We were lounging around after supper. During the meal I'd noticed Lonnie talking to Axelmann, causing him to glance up sourly from his plate a couple of times and look my way. I was about to find out why. Getting to his feet, Axelmann picked me out at once.

"I understand your boots got a bit soggy today, Daniel."

"Left, right, left, right," Greg muttered from somewhere behind me. I heard Tozer give a snort.

Axelmann pretended not to hear. Perching himself casually on a back-to-front chair, he didn't take his eyes off me. "Soggy boots. True or false?"

I shrug, say nothing.

"Brains, did your boots, or did not your boots, get a soaking?" persists Axelmann, trying to be funny.

"Simple enough question, isn't it? Too simple, per-haps? Do you want me to make it more complicated?"

Run away. Like the ripples.

"I stepped in a puddle, sir."

"A puddle, eh? A pretty big puddle, according to Lonnie here."

"Mr. Axelmann . . ." begins Lonnie from where he's sitting.

"Thank you, Warden, I can handle this." To me again. "A lake-sized puddle, to be precise."

"Yes, sir."

"He also says they were dropped into the said lake by a person or persons unknown." A pause. "Know who those persons were, do you?"

Keep running. Don't let them catch you. Not Axel-mann. None of them.

"I was swimming in the lake, sir. I was a long way away."

Axelmann gives a sigh, then looks around the room. "A mystery at sea. So—anybody here know any-thing about Daniel Edwards's diving boots?"

There's a ripple of laughter. Axelmann's lips tweak at the corners. As the laughter dies down, he looks over my head.

"Yeandle? You're squad leader. Know anything about this?"

I don't have to look around. I can see Greg's reflec-tion in the window, shaking its head slowly.

"No, sir," he lies.

"Maybe they thought they were life boots, sir?" says Flick.

More hoots of laughter. Do I imagine it, or does Tozer hoot louder than the rest? Axelmann seems to think so. He homes in on him like a hawk on its prey.

"Monkey? You have anything to do with this?"

Tozer's not like Flick, not smart enough to come out with a quip. Nor as good at lying as Greg. He just ties himself in knots.

"Me, sir? Why me?"

Axelmann slides himself from his chair and stands up.

"Because the one person Lonnie tells me he saw clearly was a person wearing an orange waterproof jacket. What color's your waterproof jacket, Monkey?"

He waits. The room falls silent.

"Orange, sir," says Tozer finally.

"The *only* orange waterproof jacket, Monkey. Because none of the others would fit a great lump like you."

No laughter this time. The atmosphere's changed. Axelmann's pacing slowly backward and forward. Everybody's looking from him to me, then back again.

I wanted to run, but he wouldn't let me.

Axelmann stops. "Yeandle," he says flatly.

"Sir?"

"This seems to be a problem confined to two members of your squad. So, they get fifty penalty points each. As Brains will tell you, that equals one hundred."

"But, sir!"

"Unless you and Harris had anything to do with it as well. In which case it'll be fifty times four—two hundred. So . . . what's it to be?"

"One hundred," says Greg at once.

He makes a beeline for me the moment Axelmann dismisses us, stands in front of me clenching and unclenching his fists. But he's not the type to lay into me. That's the sort of job he gives to Tozer. And neither of them are going to try anything straight after Axelmann's performance. Later maybe, but not now.

"We can't win best squad now," he breathes. "You're going to pay for that, Danny-boy."

You're going to pay for that, Danny-boy.

His words are still ringing in my head as I lay in my bunk, trying to sleep. At last I manage it. But, even then, my mind won't let me be.

I dream I'm on the jetty, tossing pebbles into the water, watching the ripples run away.

Run, ripples, run.

And, through it all, I'm asking myself a question I can't answer.

Where are the ripples running to?

—

"He's getting cold," I say, bending down to the unconscious figure and feeling his face.

"So what do you want me to do?" asks Tozer angrily. "Cuddle him?"

The floor of the pit is getting wetter, muddier. There's a steady trickle of water coming in now.

"He doesn't want to get too cold."

"Why? He ain't gonna die, is he?"

I feel again at the side of his neck, sense the flakes of dried blood sticking to my fingers. There's still a good pulse.

"No. I'm sure he's still okay. But if they don't come soon . . ."

Tozer swings around as I say it. "They're not going to come! This time you're wrong. They're not gonna come!"

I'm getting used to his sudden spurts of anger, his frustration. But even now, what he does catches me unawares.

He crosses to the wall beneath the ledge. Scanning the wet rock like a mountaineer, he kicks hard at a small indentation with the toe of his boot. Screwing his foot into place, he puts both arms above his head as he tries to find a grip, trying to turn his large hands into claws. With a grunt he heaves himself off the floor. He struggles for another toehold. Finding one, he moves up a fraction farther.

In my mind's eye I see him on the wall bars at school.

Monkey.

But I'm not laughing at him now. It's hopeless, he must know that. His hands are still six feet below the ledge. There's no way he can reach it, no way at all.

But I turn on my flashlight for him anyway, so that he can see better.

Again he stretches up, feeling for a place to hold on to. His fingers search across the glistening rock, probing. Suddenly he loses his grip. With a cry of rage he slithers back to the ground.

As he realizes what a small distance he'd climbed anyway, he picks up a jagged piece of rock from the floor and hurls it upward, up at the ledge, up at the shaft of light high above us.

It's as if he's gone wild. He picks up another piece, then another, hurling them up at the roof as if he's hoping they'll crack it open, oblivious to the mud and slime he's causing to rain down on us. All I can do is crouch down, covering my head with my arms, leaning over the body on the floor at the same time. When he stops, panting with the effort, he slumps to the floor. He looks across at me, still shielding the blood-stained head.

"He's gonna die. You're gonna die. All three of us. They're not coming."

"Tosh. They'll come. We'll be all right."

"He'll go first. You said he was getting cold. What if he gets that thing oldies get in the winter?"

"Hypothermia?"

"Yeh. How do you catch that?"

"You don't. It's what happens when the temperature of your body drops too low."

Even as I say it, I look up at the shaft of light,

high above us. And into my oddball mind pops another joke.

Survives one drop and dies of another!

Just like I thought I would. At the viaduct.

Chapter 11

I'd seen it as the bus swung over the hill: a viaduct, rising out of the valley beneath us, its four solid arches supporting a narrow ribbon of gravel and shale.

"Combe Viaduct," announced Mr. Redrow.

He'd been at the front of the bus since we'd left the camp, keen and enthusiastic, microphone in hand, doing a little running commentary on the scenery as we went along. This was obviously the moment he'd been waiting for.

"Constructed in 1897 from blocks of granite fifteen feet square," he gushed, "thus enabling the railway line, which ran from Combe Warren, to cross this small valley and thus extend its tentacles into the farther reaches of Blagdon and beyond . . ."

"Here, we're going train spotting!" called a voice from the back.

Mr. Redrow looked faintly embarrassed. "Ah . . . no. You won't see any trains. The line was discontinued some years ago."

"Had its tentacles cut off, so to speak, eh, Mr. Redrow?"

It's Axelmann, climbing out of his seat at the front and taking over the microphone.

The bus slows at a bend, changing gear as it begins to head downward. A gap in the trees lets us see the viaduct clearly. Somebody is working on it. Below, in the valley, two walkers look like ants.

Axelmann's in a playful mood.

"The point Mr. Redrow omitted to mention is the height of the viaduct. So—ten squad points. How high is it?"

Fifteen-foot square blocks, Redrow said. So, two across each leg. Thirty feet. Gaps between legs look twice as wide as the legs themselves. Four legs, three gaps. Four times thirty plus three times sixty. Three hundred feet across. It looks half as high as it is wide. One hundred fifty feet.

I put my hand up.

"One hundred fifty feet?"

Axelmann nods. "Bang on, Brains. Of course. One hundred fifty feet high it is." He looks at me. "Suitably impressed?"

What can I say? "Yes, sir."

"Well, here's something that'll impress you even more. You're going to jump off the top of it."

From the back I hear Greg Yeandle laugh.

As the bus wound its way down, the viaduct disappeared behind the trees. The buzz of excitement that had greeted Axelmann's announcement reaches a crescendo as the bus pulls off the road and comes to a halt.

We pile out. Axelmann leads the way, through a short tunnel of trees. On the ground the weeds have taken over, but the layers of chippings we crunch across tell us we're following the route the railway line had once taken.

Greg Yeandle smirks at me as he goes past. "All right, Danny-boy? You're looking a bit pale."

"Pale green, to be precise," says Flick, marching at his side.

Tozer simply hurries by, catching up to them, then lumbering ahead like a kid who wants to be the first to see the sea.

We come out of the tunnel of trees. Ahead, the gray and green avenue of chippings and weeds stretches forward, now with a low wall on both sides, its brickwork blackened with the smoke of a thousand trains. We're on top of the viaduct.

The person I'd seen working on it was Lonnie. He's waiting for us, a tangle of ropes and webbing at his feet. Some of the original railroad ties are still embedded in the ground. Hammered into one of them, glinting in the sun, is a large metal hook. A rope runs through it, and off over the side of the viaduct. Far below, I can see the end of the rope curled up on the valley floor, like a snoozing snake. In between, it's swinging in the breeze.

"Rappelling," announces Axelmann. "Anybody ever done it before?"

A few hands shoot up, including Yeandle's and Tozer's. Tozer's standing close by Axelmann, bursting with enthusiasm.

"Did it on vacation once," he says. "Brilliant!"

"Monkey! Of course, I should have guessed."

Laughter. Tozer grins his dumb grin, appearing not to realize that Axelmann's turned his big moment into ashes.

"Rappelling is what we're about today, gentlemen, and you're about to receive a crash course in the subject. Not literally, of course."

More laughter, but not so ready this time.

Axelmann's holding up a webbing harness, like the seat of a baby bouncer I once found when I was exploring our attic. It's got a metal hook at the front of it.

"Volunteer, please. Somebody who's done it before."

Tozer's hand shoots up. Axelmann looks through him.

"Yeandle."

Greg steps forward. Axelmann uses him as a dummy while he talks.

"What will happen is that you'll put this harness on, like so. It joins at the front. Now, see this?" He waggles the hook at the front of the harness, at Greg's waist. "It's called a carabiner."

He takes the end of the rope Lonnie hands him.

"This rope passes through the carabiner, which acts as a brake. Pull it like so"—he shows how—"and it lets the rope through. Close it again, and the rope stops. Everybody got that?"

A few nods, some uncertain.

"Now, there's absolutely nothing that can go wrong," says Axelmann.

He runs his hands back from Greg's waist, feeding the rope through them until he reaches a second carabiner. "This is your guarantee, okay? I'll be operating this carabiner. I can use it to stop your descent at any time."

He looks around. "Any questions?"

Everything goes quiet. Then I hear a voice. Mine.

"Why do we have to do this?"

It's as if I'm a magnet as faces swing around to look my way. Greg Yeandle smirks, Tozer grins his dumb grin, Flick Harris groans. But am I wrong, or do some of the others seem pleased the question's been asked?

Not Axelmann, though. He sniffs, turns to look over the side of the viaduct, at the dangling rope. For a minute I think he's not going to answer at all. Then he turns back again. He's oozing patience.

"Edwards, we're—you're—doing this because it's going to teach you something more about trust. Look at it this way . . ."

He's toying with the carabiner, the one he called our guarantee.

". . . It's a bit like going into a hospital when you're

ill. You can't make yourself better, so you have to put your trust in the doctors and nurses. Well, in this exercise I'm your doctor. I'm going to look after you and make sure you don't break your little neck. Got that? Team members trust one another."

He's talking to the whole group now, as if my question's been dealt with.

"For this exercise, I'm a member of your team. You have to trust me. It's as simple as that. Right?"

Nobody has a chance to answer, even if he'd been looking for one. He ushers Greg Yeandle toward the viaduct wall, the rest of us into a line alongside it.

I look over the top. Mr. Lomax and Mr. Redrow are down in the valley at the base of the central pillar, one hundred fifty feet below, like fielders waiting for a catch.

One hundred fifty feet.

I'm oblivious to what's going on—to Yeandle being helped up onto the viaduct wall and over the side, to the others cheering him on.

All I can see is the ground, far below. One hundred fifty feet below.

One hundred fifty feet. The same height as A-Block, with the school library at the top.

I see Tozer fluttering my pages out of the window, my calculations.

My calculations. A body dropped from 150 feet up would hit the ground at sixty miles an hour.

I see me gathering the pages together again.

Pages flutter, get slowed down by the wind. But a brick wouldn't. A body wouldn't. I wouldn't.

"Yehh!"

A roar of triumph. Far below, on the ground, Greg is being released from the harness. His excited voice flies upward.

"Easy!"

The line moves forward as the others go over the side and on down, feet on the blackened bricks, leaning back like sailors balancing a yacht.

Some, those who've done it before—like Tozer— go quickly, bouncing lightly down in short horizontal hops.

Others go slowly, clinging to the taut rope, their faces white with fear.

And all the while there's that voice in my head, reciting the same number over and over again.

Sixty miles an hour. Sixty, sixty, sixty . . .

"You next, Brains."

I'm at the front of the line.

I stand rigid as Axelmann puts the harness on me. Two straps around my legs, a belt around my waist. I look down at them. Close up, I see the straps are worn. Little strands of webbing are sticking out of the sides.

Can it hold me? Will it hold me? Sixty miles an hour.

The carabiner's jutting out in front of me. Axelmann's repeating the business about braking, sliding the rope backward and forward through it. I see the tiny hairs of frayed rope passing over the dull metal, and I'm not listening to what he's saying.

Sixty miles an hour.

"I don't want to do it."

The words just come out. I can hear myself saying them, so Axelmann must hear them too. He pretends not to.

"Up you go."

"Come on, Danny-boy. Let's see you dangle."

It's Greg Yeandle. Flick and Tozer are standing with him. They've taken the trouble to climb all the way back up for this.

There's a brick missing on the inside of the viaduct wall. Axelmann puts my foot in the gap, as if it's a stirrup and I'm about to climb on a horse.

"Up," he says.

He holds me tight as I swing my leg over the top of the wall. I feel the rough bricks beneath me. "Right. Sit there for a minute." He gives the rope at my waist another fiddle.

"Now look," he says, leaning over the wall and pointing a little way down. There's a narrow ledge by my foot. It runs the length of the viaduct. "See that ledge? I want you to climb over slowly, so you're standing on it."

"Don't fall, though," calls Yeandle.

Sixty miles an hour.

"When you're there," Axelmann's saying, "let the

rope take your weight. Lean out. Then, when you're ready, start walking backward."

"But don't look down, Danny-boy," calls Greg. "It's a long way to the bottom."

One hundred fifty feet. Sixty miles an hour.

"I don't want to do it."

Again, it's as if I've not said it.

"Shut up, Yeandle," snaps Axelmann. Then, to me, "Do it."

"No. If I fall . . ."

"You won't fall. Nobody's going to let you fall. Trust me."

Trust him?

Trust him? Remember Axelmann putting his foot behind Tozer's heels? Remember the shove? You can't trust him, Daniel. Ever.

"I'm not doing it. I'm not doing it!"

"Edwards . . ."

"No!"

"Oh, dear," calls Yeandle. "Looks like another wet boots job."

"Chicken," calls Tozer, "the Weirdo's chicken."

"Tozer! Shut up! Edwards . . ."

But I'm already on my way back down from the top of the wall, leaning, slipping, falling to the safety of the ground at Axelmann's feet. He stares down at me. There's a piece of chewing gum jammed between his teeth.

"Gutless," he breathes. "Get up. You're going to go down if I . . ."

"He doesn't have to do it." A voice from behind him. Quiet. It's Lonnie.

Axelmann spins around to face him. "He does have to do it!"

Lonnie doesn't raise his voice, just says again, "He does not."

"He does!" yells Axelmann. There are flecks of spit at the corner of his mouth. "He has to do it! For his own sake!"

He jabs a finger in the direction of Yeandle and the others.

"You know what they call him? Do you? Know what they think of him? If he does this, he might just earn their respect. They might just accept him as one of them instead of thinking he's a . . ."

"He does not have to do it," says Lonnie again. This time, though, he says it with an edge of steel in his voice that can't be missed. I sense he's not going to let Axelmann steamroller his way over him like he did at the boots interrogation.

Axelmann senses it too. He pauses. He's breathing hard. He starts chewing again.

Then he's pulling the harness off me, not even looking at me as he does it. When he's finished, he turns to Greg, all sarcasm.

"Yeandle. A member of your squad appears not to

be in a rappelling mood today. So, you have a problem. Understand? *You* have a problem. How is he going to get down to the bottom?"

Greg shrugs. "Fly?"

Axelmann doesn't give a hint of a smile. Greg spots the warning sign. "Don't know, sir," he adds quickly.

"Perhaps I can make a suggestion, then. Carry him down between you."

"Mr. Axelmann . . ." It's Lonnie. "That's not the answer."

Axelmann swings around on him. He's not going to lose this one. "My decision, Lonnie. Okay? Edwards doesn't have to rappel, but he *does* have to go down."

"Not that way."

"I disagree. We're about teamwork this week, are we not? About trust, about looking after each other? All admirable qualities, wouldn't you say?"

Before Lonnie can reply he snaps his fingers at Greg, Flick, and Tozer; jerks his head toward me. "Carry him. Down to the bottom."

"I can walk down," I say.

Now he turns on me. Every word he spits out tells me what he thinks, that I'm the lowest of the low.

"You want to be a passenger, Brains? Fine, you be a passenger. But passengers are carried." Then, to the other three, "Now, pick him up!"

Tozer hooks his big hands under my arms. Yeandle and Harris take a leg each. Between them, they cart me off the viaduct and around the widening track leading down the embankment and into the valley below.

Axelmann walked behind us every step of the way, saying nothing as they puffed and panted, dug their fingers into me as they altered their grip, bounced me on the ground as they slithered down the steeper parts.

You know what it's like in a dentist's chair? The way you look anywhere except into the dentist's eyes? That's how it was.

I couldn't look at them. I just stared at the sky, at the bank of gray clouds coming over, at the vapor trail a jet was making high above the clouds—stared as hard as I could.

Maybe that's what made my eyes water. All I know is, they needed wiping by the time we reached the bottom and they let me go.

"Mind if I join you?"

Lonnie hadn't waited for me to answer yes or no. He'd just settled himself down beside me on the jetty. After we'd got back from the viaduct I'd left them to it, left them to their jeering and cheering, and headed for the lake again.

"Want to talk about it?" he says.

"About what?"

"The rappelling."

"There's nothing to say about it, is there? I didn't do it."

Clouds are scudding in from the west, gathering above Ebbor Down as if that's where they'd agreed to meet.

"Being frightened isn't a crime, you know."

I shrug. "Tell that to Axelmann."

Lonnie sighs, gently. "I don't think that your Mr. Axelmann would understand. He's the type who thinks fear is a sign of weakness."

Run, ripples, run.

"Well, isn't it?" I say, suddenly angry. "I was running away, wasn't I? Like the ripples . . ."

I snatch up a small piece of rock, ready to throw it into the lake. But as I pull my arm back, Lonnie grips my wrist tight. He pries the rock from my hand.

Then, like before, what he says next seems irrelevant.

"Do you know what this stuff is?"

He's toying with the piece of rock, turning it in his hand. He looks at me.

I shrug, shake my head. "Rock? Rock's rock, isn't it?"

"No, it isn't. This is limestone. It's the same type of rock you saw in the Cheddar Gorge."

I look more closely at the piece of rock in his hand. It's dark gray, nothing special. I try to think of it multiplied a billion times into the steep sheer walls of the gorge.

"Daniel," he says. "How do you think the gorge was formed?"

It was as if we were passing through a gap made by some god from Greek mythology, a god who'd swung an ax and sliced the hill in two . . .

"Earthquake," I say.

Lonnie shakes his head. "Water," he says simply. "Melting snow. Torrents of it, running down from the Mendip Hills as the Ice Age came to an end. Water finding its own level, Daniel . . ."

He points out toward the rock faces on the other side of the lake and the spread of Ebbor Down above them.

"It's the same over there, you know, except you can't see it. The core of Ebbor Down is sandstone. But around the outside, the part you can see"—he holds up the piece of rock again—"limestone."

"So?"

He looks at me with his steady gaze. "What do you know about limestone, Daniel?"

I shrug. "I don't get you."

"This rock," he says, holding his hand out. "Is it tough? Strong?"

"It looks it."

"It looks it, Daniel. But it isn't as tough as it looks. You know what rainwater does to this stuff?"

"What?"

"It dissolves it. Oh, it takes a long time, but the water wins in the end."

He's bouncing the piece of limestone up and down in his hand.

"Why do you think this place is called Combe Warren, Daniel? Because although those rocks over there look strong, inside them it's like a rabbit warren. The water's eating its way through them, finding its level. Year in, year out, every time it rains. And when there's a storm . . ."

He shakes his head, as if remembering.

"Daniel, the water can come off the Down and into those caves with a power more frightening than you've ever seen. Water, angry water, knowing where its level is and letting nothing stand in its way."

Suddenly he turns and tosses the lump of limestone out into the lake. A mushroom of water shoots up, and then the ripples begin.

Run, ripples, run.

"You said you were like those ripples, Daniel. Running away. Yes?"

I nod.

Lonnie's looking at me, bending to meet my eyes. "Daniel. Don't you see? They're not running away."

Out on the water the ripples are fading, slowly vanishing.

"Daniel, they're going back to where they started. Going back for more."

I see then what he's driving at. At least I think I do.

"Going back? That's what you're telling me to do, is it? Just put up with it? Just keep on going back for more of the same?"

"Yes, it is," he says quietly.

"I can't."

"I think you can. I think you're strong enough. Strong, like the water."

"Strong?" I yell. "Running back for more? That's not strong! It's stupid! I can't win that war! I'll never beat them!"

Wordlessly, Lonnie looks away from me and toward the lake. Its surface is smooth again. The ripples have gone.

"I can see the water, Daniel. But where is the rock?"

Chapter 12

Survives one drop and dies of another!

It's only when the daft joke flits out of my mind that I notice it.

"Look! The ledge!"

Even as I say the words, I'm thinking that they're actually pretty stupid. There's no ledge up there for Tozer to look at. Not anymore. That's the whole point. Now, picked out in the shaft of light high above us, it's been reduced to no more than a jagged lip of rock jutting out from the wall.

"Where's it gone?" asks Tozer.

There's only one explanation. I point at the muck and rubble that fell down during Tozer's mad fit of rock throwing.

"You must have done it."

"Come on," says Tozer. "Who do you think I am, Superman? I couldn't have done that. It must have been ready to come down."

As he says it something clicks into place. I look at

the figure on the ground, remember the last thing I heard him say.

"Watch out. It's slippery in here."

I scrabble in my backpack, pull out my flashlight, switch it on, turn its strong beam upward toward what I'd thought was a blacker patch of rock. Now, with the help of the shaft of light coming from the entrance, I can see it.

"Look! Above where the ledge was."

"What?"

"There! It's a hole!"

Above the lip of rock, visible now that the ledge is no longer there, is a round hole in the side of the wall. It extends almost up to the roof. Tozer looks up as I explain what I've just realized.

"That must be a passageway. That's the way it was. This isn't just a pit we've fallen into."

I look again at the source of the shaft of light, much higher up on the opposite side—at what was the entrance. Trickles of water are oozing between the rocks. And, now that I'm looking for it, I think I can make out the ragged remains of another ledge.

"That hole," I say. "From the entrance the ground must have sloped down to there. But it must have been weak. Just waiting for somebody to tread on it. With this place beneath it all the time."

Like the cavity in a rotten tooth.

"You're saying that's a tunnel. It could be a way out? You saying that?"

He brings me up short. I wasn't trying to raise his hopes, just explain the solution to a puzzle I've solved. But, of course, he doesn't see it that way.

"So how do we reach it! Come on? How do we get up there?"

The sound of his voice bounces off the wet walls and echoes up into the roof of the cave.

"Come on! You're the brains around here! How do we get up there!"

"I don't know," is all I can say.

Now it's my turn to fall silent, admit defeat by saying nothing.

And, this time, it's Tozer who breaks the silence. He doesn't sound angry. He speaks slowly, as if he's trying to think it out for himself as he says it.

"You wanted to know why I give you such a hard time."

I look at him. "Yes. Why?"

"I never thought about it before. When you asked a while back it threw me." He lets out a breath. "You know what I reckon?"

"What?"

"I'm jealous of you."

Jealous? Of a weirdo?

He goes on, quietly, his voice low in the dark. "I reckon we all are. I know I am."

Tozer gives a half laugh. "I know it's why I didn't want to be stuck with you on the orienteering."

I turn toward him.

"Stuck with me? Tosh, you had no chance. You were always going to be stuck with me."

I gesture across the floor of our prison. "He knew that."

—

The maps had been spread out, waiting for us, in the big hut. One map to a cabin squad, one squad to a table.

Did it really only happen this morning?

Axelmann prowled up and down, waiting until we were settled. There was no sign of Lonnie.

Why Lonnie? That was when it occurred to me—why did he like to be called Lonnie?

Redrow and Lomax were at the front, looking helpful, sifting papers. At Axelmann's nod, Lomax handed him one of the sheets while Redrow popped up and started giving out the rest, one per table.

"This afternoon," said Axelmann, still prowling, "you will be engaging in the noble activity of orienteering. That is, finding your way around the countryside by means of your wits, your legs—and teamwork. The sheet of paper Mr. Redrow has just given to each squad leader tells you where you've got to find your way around to."

He waits for the shuffling to die down as the pages are inspected.

"It gives the map references for seven markers, A to G. You've got to visit each marker and discover the code number that's on it. You'll have two hours, not a minute more. Squads have to go out together, visit all the markers, and come back together. So—start planning your routes."

At first there's a small period of quiet as Axelmann's words sink in. Then the chair moving and talking begins.

Greg Yeandle assumes command, turning our map around so that it's in front of him. Flick shuffles his chair to Yeandle's elbow. Tozer can get no nearer than the side of the table. He kneels on his chair, twisting his head around so that he doesn't have to read upside down.

I sit opposite Greg. It's the only place left, after all. He works through the sheet of seven map references, marking each on the map with a circle and its letter. The result reminds me of one of those dot-to-dot puzzles, one that looks like it's going to end up as a heart.

From where we are, markers A, B, and C bulge out to the north and west. Markers D, E, and F are opposite, bulging out to the north and east to skirt the lake. The seventh marker, G, dips down about equidistant between C and F, but south of them both.

"Okay, these are the places we've got to visit," says Greg. "All we've got to do now is work out the best route."

Tozer leans across the map. "Go to A first," he says, tracing an as-the-crow-flies line with his thumb. "That's nearest."

"You're right, Tosh!" says Flick, all enthusiastic.

"Yeh?"

Flick examines the map closely. "I mean, it can't be more than, what—a couple of inches? Shouldn't take long at all, not with feet your size."

Greg shoves him out of the way, then looks up at Tozer.

"Tosher, do us a favor. Check to see if your brain's at home before opening the front door." He dabs at the map. "Look at those contour lines."

On the map there's a finger of closely packed contour lines poking into the space between the starting point and marker A.

"They mean there's a big hill there," says Flick. "A . . . big . . . hill. You know, like in Jack and Jill? Your old lady still tell you that one, does she?"

"'Grand Old Duke of York,' more like," scoffs Greg. "And Tosher's the duke. He wants to march us up to the top of the hill and march us down again." He jabs at the map. "That's the way we'll go. Around the bottom of the hill."

Tozer looks, but doesn't understand. "Why? Longer, isn't it?"

Greg sighs loudly. "It may be farther, but it'll be quicker."

"In the long run, ho-ho," says Flick.

Tozer sinks back onto his seat like a flat tire. Yeandle plots on, measuring distances and working out the quickest route around all seven markers. He's good, all right. Smart. But he's missed something.

Finally, he sits back. "Right, that's it then. That's the way we go. All agreed?"

Flick nods.

Tozer sits up and gives the map a blank look. "Go for it. Why not?"

Yeandle puts his hand up, looking for Axelmann to come over and give his seal of approval.

"Route all right with you, Danny-boy?" he says over his shoulder.

I shrug, say nothing . . .

Run, ripples, run.

. . . until Yeandle smirks at Flick as he adds, "I've avoided all the viaducts."

Then, suddenly, I'm angry and all I can hear is Lonnie's voice pounding in my brain . . .

I can see the water, Daniel. But where is the rock?

. . . and all I want to do is to drown Greg Yeandle, drown him in any way I can.

"No," I snap. "The route's not all right with me. It won't work."

Yeandle's hand comes down like a shot. "What do you mean, it won't work?" he says, smirk wiped off.

"Two hours, Axelmann said. That route's too far to cover in the time."

He stares at me for a few seconds, then goes back to his figures. "Nine miles," he says, finally. "We can run that in two hours."

"Run?" says Flick. "You are joking, my friend!"

Yeandle's face goes even tighter as Flick adds to his

misery. "Anyway, it's not just getting there, is it? We've got to find those markers as well. Knowing Axelmann, he'll probably have them behind bushes and up trees."

"Scummer," growls Tozer.

Yeandle turns to me then, all charm. "So what do you reckon, Dan? What's the answer?"

I give it to him. "Split up."

"What?"

I trace the route on his map with my finger, following the two sides of the heart shape.

"Two go to markers A, B, and C"—I trace around the west side of the balloon shape on his map, then the eastern side—"while the others go to D, E, and F."

Yeandle's face creases into a victory scowl. "Haven't you forgotten something, Danny-boy? Axie said we've all got to go together."

Sink, Yeandle. Down you go.

"No, he didn't. What he actually said was, 'Squads have to go out together, visit all the markers, and come back together.' He didn't say we have to stay together all the way around."

I point at the last marker, in the center of the heart shape. He looks as if it's his own heart I'm poking my finger into as I say, "We meet up again at marker G, then come back together." I stare straight into his eyes. "I think it's called teamwork."

Flick is nodding slowly. "He's right, y'know. That'd only be about four miles each. Easy enough in two hours."

"Well done, Danny-boy," says Greg, tight faced. Slowly he puts his hand up again.

Axelmann breezes over straight away. "Well, what's the plan. Don't tell me, you're all going to hang on to Monkey's legs as he swings through the trees."

Yeandle pushes the map forward and points out the markers he's drawn in. Axelmann glances at them quickly.

"So, what's your route going to be? You're too far behind to win best squad, but if you get this right you might not end up in last place."

"We're . . . we're going to split up. Take three markers each and meet up at the last."

"Excellent," glows Axelmann, "excellent. Whose idea was that?"

Yeandle doesn't look my way. "Team discussion," he says.

"Okay," says Axelmann. "Yeandle, come and get another map from me. You'll have to mark it up so that both pairs have got one."

He looks hard around the table. "Pairs, you hear me? I don't want any solo efforts. I'm not having one of you lot wandering the countryside on your own. So, who's going with who?"

"We haven't sorted that out yet," says Greg.

"Well, I know who I *don't* want to go with," Tozer mutters, glancing my way.

Axelmann turns on him. "The other three are probably saying the same about you, Monkey."

For once, Tozer's dumb grin doesn't appear.

"Well, I'm sure I can leave team selection in your capable hands, Yeandle." Axelmann turns to go, then stops. "Better keep Monkey happy, though. Toss up for partners. Or play spuds, eh?"

In my mind's eye I see him, looking through our cabin window during the beds debate.

"Spuds?" echoes Greg. "Good idea, sir. Spuds it is. Okay, Tosher?"

—

Tozer's voice comes back at me in the dark.

"What do you mean, I had no chance?"

"Just that. It was always going to be you and me."

"But we played spuds."

"I know you played spuds. That's the whole point! It's a game that never changes."

"I don't get it . . ."

"Then think about it! Remember? Why did he start with you? Why did he start with you when you were arguing about the beds? Because with spuds it's always going to work out the same. Where you start decides where you finish."

In the dark, above the steady sound of trickling water, I hear Tozer breathing noisily, in and out, in and out, as if it's an effort picturing the scene in his head . . .

Greg Yeandle saying, "Spuds up, Tosh. First out between you and Flick goes with Danny-boy. Fair enough?"

Greg Yeandle sounding as though he means it when he says, "I hope I get you, Tosher. Flick's a real pain."

Greg Yeandle starting with Tozer's right fist, then his left, "One potato, two potato . . ."

"So—it was a fix?" asks Tozer blankly.

"He was making sure you got stuck with me? Yes."

Tozer swears, clearly and loudly.

Then murmurs, almost under his breath, "Yeandle, if we get out of here . . ."

I think he's losing hope. We've been down here three hours now.

And he didn't say, "When we get out of here . . ."
He said, "If."

Chapter 13

We'd been gathered together at the starting point, a sprawling oak tree.

"Looks like rain," said Greg Yeandle, eyeing the sky. He looked down at my boots and exchanged glances with Flick. "Been a bit of a wet week all around, what with one thing and another."

"Ah, well," said Flick out of Tozer's earshot. "What d'you expect when you've a couple of drips in your squad?"

Axelmann was bustling about, asking questions, not listening to the answers.

"Got your rain gear? Everybody got their whistles?"

A flurry of peeps, like a dozen referees practicing.

"All right, all right. You've got those whistles for a reason. If you get lost or separated from your squad—use them." A nod toward Lonnie, standing patiently at one side. "Lonnie and I will be checking the area all the time. So, if you do get lost, stay put and keep blowing your whistle. Sooner or later, one of us will hear you."

I check the right-hand pocket of my backpack. Whistle and flashlight. *Right for life.*

Axelmann takes a final look around, stops as he spots Tozer. Everybody's got his compass strung around his neck except him.

"Monkey! Where's your compass?"

Tozer digs in his jacket pocket and pulls out his compass, holding it up by its red string.

"Not much good to you in there, is it?" yells Axelmann. "Put it around your neck—and use it. With a bit of luck it might stop you going around in circles and disappearing up your own . . ."

Laughter drowns the final muttered word. Tozer gives his usual dumb grin.

"Right," yells Axelmann. "Away you go."

The moment we're off, Tozer shoves the compass straight back into his pocket.

Yeandle's in the lead, holding the map, Flick at his side, as we head toward the splitting point. They seem in no great hurry. Me neither. I tag along behind, counting my steps and using them to check the distance we've gone.

"Going a bit slow, ain't we?" says Tozer, turning around. He's fashioned a golf club out of a dead branch and has been stalking ahead, using it to slash at the bracken as he goes.

"No hurry, Tosher," says Yeandle. "We're not in the running for top squad."

"So we're not running," says Flick.

The track curves right through a grassy hollow. My compass needle turns as we follow the track around.

"Thar she blows, skipper!" shouts Flick.

Ahead of us the track forks in two. Greg looks at me. It's the first time he's acknowledged my existence since we started.

"So—time for the parting of the ways then?" he says, no-teeth smile. "Ready, Flick?" Then louder, to Tozer, who's still playing games, "See you later, Tosh."

Tozer doesn't answer, just thrashes wildly at an overhanging branch. Yeandle makes to leave.

"Map?" I say.

"You what?"

"Map. You did get another one from Axelmann?"

"Oh, yeh." He slips his backpack from his shoulders, takes out another of Axelmann's maps. He hands it to me. The seven markers are drawn in, one thick cross for each. Their grid references are listed in the margin.

"One I prepared earlier, Danny-boy," he says.

I glance at it, at the seven crosses. Heart-shaped pattern. Seen the right way up, the pattern looks slightly different, seems to have a bit more of a bulge on the side we're going to be following. And we've dawdled enough this far. We could be pushed for time.

As he heads off with Flick at his side, Yeandle gives a last call over his shoulder. "See you at the last marker. Don't get lost, now!"

And then, as if it's happened suddenly, there's just the two of us. And the silence.

That's when I realize: there's no Greg, no Flick. No Axelmann. No audience. It's the first time Tozer and I have ever been alone together.

I don't know what to say to him.

Tozer doesn't seem to know what to say to me either. Until now he's been babbling and prattling about anything and nothing. Now he seems to have run dry.

He thrashes idly at the bracken, not looking my way. It's then I realize something else. He's more bothered about the situation than I am.

"You want the map?" I say.

He shakes his head, waits, kicking idly at the end of the branch in his hand.

I start walking. He follows, keeping his distance.

The track peters out inside three hundred feet, just as the map shows. By my reckoning we want to head northeast. I check this, laying my compass on the map and taking a bearing on an earthwork I can see. It confirms my thinking.

"This way, yes?" I say, pointing to a narrow pathway threading through the trees.

Tozer shrugs, says nothing, just follows in silence

until I stop again. I hold the map out toward him, my finger in place.

"That cart track should be up here. See where it bends? If we go there we should be able to use a compass to find marker D." I show him Yeandle's cross, the bold letter D beside it, just to the west. "It shouldn't be more than one hundred feet away from there."

Again, it looks as if he's going to ignore me. Then, suddenly, he swings around.

"I don't want to see it. All right? You're the brains. I'll follow you."

He's trying to be his usual weirdo-baiting self, but he's not making it. There's something about the way he's acting I haven't seen before.

He's nervous. More nervous than me. What we're doing is all about angles and measurements—and he can't handle it. Sink, Tozer! Drown, Tozer!

"Come on, then," I say. "It's this way."

The cart track is just where I expect it to be, bending like an elbow from north to east. He stops as I stop, standing at the elbow to take a bearing with my compass.

"Over there," I say, pointing toward a thick wall of shrubs and brambles.

"I can't see anything."

I ignore him now. Holding my compass out in front of me, I walk on in the direction I've worked out, eyes focused on the moving needle, counting my steps. He follows.

"Well, where is it?" asks Tozer as we get to the shrubbery.

"There's another fifty feet to go. It must be behind this lot."

I look from side to side. There seems no easy way through until Tozer turns around and backs through a small gap, ducking down as the branches harmlessly bounce off his shoulders instead of slicing into his face as they would if he'd gone in headfirst.

Practical. Why couldn't I think of that?

This time, I follow him.

"Typical." It's Tozer, sounding pleased and scornful at the same time. "Typical Axelmann."

He's standing beside marker D, placed in a small open space behind the shrubbery, impossible to see from the other side.

"Two-two-eight" he says, bending down to read out the code number. He looks up at me. "Pretty good," he says. "Greg will be pleased."

And he actually smiles . . .

—

It's getting darker again. High above us the shaft of light is growing dimmer. It seems as if our hope is fading with it.

"Reckon we're right out of it now, eh?" says Tozer suddenly. "*Vulture* squad? Had a bit more than our two hours, ain't we?"

He moves close to me. I feel him shiver. "Poor old Greg. He's not used to losing."

"You should know. He's your friend."

He doesn't say anything for a moment. In the gap I hear, from far above, the low rumble of thunder.

Then he says, "He's not."

"What?"

"Greg. He's not my friend. Not really. Nor Flick."

I laugh. "They were! Before they cheated you into getting stuck with me!"

"No, they weren't. They never have been. Not *real* friends. They're real friends with each other. Not with me. I haven't got any real friends."

So, join the club!

"Is that why you're always at me, then?" I ask. There's no anger anymore. I just want to know. "Trying to impress them? Turn them into your friends?"

"No. Well . . . yeh, I suppose that's part of it. Not all of it. I told you. I'm jealous of you."

"You didn't say why."

"Ain't it obvious?"

"No, it's not."

I click on my flashlight, but this time shine it up at my own face.

"Hey, look. Remember me? Weirdo? Why should you be jealous of me? What have I got that you want?"

His answer hits me like a bullet.

"Brains," he says simply.

I don't know what to say. All I can do is turn off my flashlight again, hope he'll be the next to speak.

"Nobody says so. But, if you ask me, all of us envy you in that way. Greg, Flick—even Axelmann, I reckon. I don't know who he hates more, me because I'm stupid or you because you're not."

"I don't understand," I say, and I'm being honest.

"*You* don't understand? I like it!" His laugh rattles around the walls. "Here, listen everybody! Monkey's discovered something Brains don't understand!"

Then, softly, he says, "You got any idea what it's like for me? Eh? Sitting there, looking at a book, not understanding a word of it? You got any idea what that's like?"

"Of course I have. I don't understand a lot of stuff at first."

"Yeh, at first. But that's the difference, ain't it? You might not understand something at first, but you know if you really have a go at it you'll get there in the end. Me, I know I won't. Even if I sit and stare at it till my head feels like it's gonna come off, I know I won't *ever* understand."

A memory, fresh, less than a few hours old, comes back to me.

"That's not true, Tosh. What about the compass? You understood about that."

"Oh, yeh. The compass."

He spits the words out, as though they're a taste he wants to get rid of. "The compass," he says again. "And look where that got us. Down here!"

"No, it didn't!" I shout. For the first time in my life I actually want to help Tozer, give him something to feel good about.

Again I snap on my flashlight, aim the beam down at the cold form lying on the floor.

"He got us down here! Not you. Not me. Him!"

Chapter 14

After finding marker D, I could sense that Tozer's mood had changed somehow, softened in some way. As I studied the map he was a bit more interested.

"Where to now, then?"

"Head for that bridge."

I'm showing him the map, and the stream running not far from where Greg Yeandle has drawn in marker E. A small bridge is nearby.

"Why not go straight there?"

His finger draws a line between where we are and marker E. My route is going to take us around in an arc.

"Safety first," I say. "If we follow the track, then aim for something we can see easily, there's less chance we'll get lost. And it's quicker."

"How come?"

"We don't have to keep checking our direction with the compass."

He puts a hand into his pocket and pulls out the

compass he'd shoved in there after Axelmann's go at him at the starting point. Even though he's looking at it as though it's a foreign object, I don't see the obvious.

"We can try it straight there with the compass, if you want," I say.

"No. We'll go your way."

He falls silent again as we set off, says nothing until we come out from the trees and see the tiny gray drystone bridge ahead of us.

"Now what?" he asks as we reach it.

"Now we take a compass bearing on marker E from the map."

"In English, eh?"

It's the blindfold business all over again. What's obvious to me is a mystery to him. I surprise myself, and remember not the pain of that day but the lesson I learned.

"According to the map, marker E should be over there somewhere." I point away toward a stretch of open ground, dotted with trees and leading up toward a rise. "All I have to do is set up the compass again, just like I did before. It'll take us straight to it."

He looks uncertain for a minute, as if he's wrestling with a problem. Then he's fishing in his pocket and pulling out his own compass.

"So how d'you use this thing, anyway?"

"You don't know?"

Idiot. Of course he doesn't know. Why'd he stuff it away

when Axelmann mentioned it? Why hasn't he wanted to talk until now?

He shrugs. "Wouldn't be asking if I did, would I?"

I want you to sink, Tozer. I want you to sink to the bottom. So why can't I push you under?

I hand the map to him. He takes it gingerly, almost as if it's alive. I point to the bridge we're standing at, then Yeandle's cross for marker E.

"Okay. Put your compass on it so that the long edge joins the bridge to marker E."

Tozer shifts the compass so that its edge is against the middle of Yeandle's cross. Then he jiggles the other end until it's against the bridge symbol.

"Keep it steady. Now, turn the dial until that arrow points straight up at the top of the map."

He turns the dial slowly, his tongue unconsciously clamped between his teeth. He glances at me when he's done it, as if looking for approval. I take the map from him, leaving him with the compass.

"What . . ."

"You don't need the map for this bit. Just hold the compass out in front of you." He does it. "Now, turn yourself around until the red end of the needle points the same way as the arrow."

Step by step, Tozer shuffles around. The compass needle swings in little jerks until he stops with it quivering over the orienting arrow.

"Now look straight ahead. Marker E is that way."

He stands stock still, staring toward the rise. "You mean . . . if I just walk—I'll come to it?"

"If you make sure the compass needle stays over the arrow all the time—yes."

He looks at the compass, clamped between his fingers. "And that's it? That's all there is to it?"

It's all about angles, Tozer. Geometry. Weirdo things, you know? No, of course you don't. I realize that now.

"Only one way to find out," I say. "Give it a go."

We set off, toward the rise, Tozer's eyes bobbing up and down from the compass to where we're headed. As we come over the rise, the ground falls away in front of us toward a grassy knoll in the distance.

"I can't see it," he says. "It isn't here. I've got it wrong, haven't I?"

"There's still a few hundred feet to go."

He starts off again, walking faster, his head going up and down to check the compass. As we reach the knoll he scampers to the top—and stops dead.

"It's there! Look! Look! It's there!"

Axelmann's placed the red and white marker on the other side of the knoll. Tozer's just standing there, looking down at it as if it's the eighth wonder of the world.

"You want to get the code number?" I say.

He doesn't move, doesn't answer, doesn't say a thing until I begin to slide down the other side of the knoll to make a note of the code number.

Then he's not talking to me, but to himself. Over and over again.

"I got it right. I got it right . . ."

By the time I'd checked the marker and come back, he was down at the bottom of the knoll himself.

"One left," he says. He's already checked the map and now he's turning like a robot, compass in front of him, to find the direction bearing we need. "That way," he says, looking up.

I swear if I hadn't said, "Hold on a minute," he'd have been off.

Instead, he stands by impatiently as I look at the map and Greg Yeandle's bold cross for marker F. It's northwest of where we are now, sitting between two whorls of contour lines, like a pair of crossed strips of bacon between two fried eggs.

The upper fried egg is by far the largest. It's the bulk of Ebbor Down, the lines within lines showing its rise up to the direction beacon at its top.

Below Yeandle's cross, the contour lines of the lower fried egg don't make it all the way around, but fall into a patch of blue—the lake.

From the map details I try to picture the place in my mind's eye: a small valley, with the bulk of Ebbor Down rising up on one side, and the opposite incline— as invisible from the jetty as the dark side of the moon—leading to the edge of the lake's rock walls on the other.

"Come on," says Tozer. "What're we waiting for? If we get this one fast, we can be back at the meeting place before Greg and Flick get there."

So that's it. That's what the hurry is. It's his big chance. His chance to show them, maybe even show Axelmann.

And, as I think about it, I realize that Tozer isn't the only one who fancies getting to the meeting point before the other two.

I can see the water, Daniel. But where's the rock?

"Come on, Tosh," I say. "Let's go for it."

It's not until we're on the way that I realize it's the first time I've ever called him by his nickname.

The feeling that something was wrong started creeping up on me even before we reached the place we were aiming for.

Although we hadn't seen anybody else on our way around, we'd heard them. Catcalls, wolf whistles, owl hoots. Either that, or we'd seen evidence of their passing—a candy wrapper, a crumpled up ball of paper.

Now, as we skirt around the base of Ebbor Down, it seems that we're the only ones around.

The feeling grows as we start to come down, taking it slowly, trying not to put a foot into one of the patchwork of grooves and crevices in the ground.

"Must be down there, eh?" says Tozer, pointing.

Valley, I now see, isn't the right word for the place Yeandle's cross has brought us to. It's more of a shallow gully, a flat, narrow avenue between two steady inclines of growth-covered rock.

It's an avenue that is scored with grooves, too, running across it like scars, growing deeper and wider as they descend from Ebbor Down. But an avenue that's clear, for all that.

And I can't see the marker.

I follow Tozer as he half runs, half slithers the final one hundred feet down to the gully floor. The avenue leads away to our left and right, a tree here, a mound there.

And still I can't see the marker.

"Where is it?" he says.

"I don't know," I say. "It doesn't—"

"What? Doesn't what?"

"It doesn't look right."

He swings around, his face a mix of doubt and rage. "You mean I've got it wrong."

"No, that's not what I mean! We're definitely in the right place."

Slowly, as if he still doesn't believe me, Tozer looks around.

"Then where's the marker?"

He begins to move about, kicking at things, peering into the greenery growing out of the rocks, like a golfer looking for a lost ball.

I follow him around, thinking maybe one of the other squads has hidden it as a joke. But there's nowhere obvious.

Tozer leads us deeper into the gully.

"This is too far," I say.

"I want to find it!" he shouts.

I check my watch.

"Look—we've got two out of three. That's not bad. If we're going to meet the others we're going to have to move."

"No."

"We'll be late. Axelmann will go nuts."

"Stuff Axelmann. Stuff them all." He turns to me and I can see he's deadly serious. "I'm going nowhere till I find that marker . . ."

It was the first flash of lightning that stopped him looking. Then the thunder, rolling toward us from the storm clouds that had been slowly gathering above Ebbor Down. We'd been searching for the best part of an hour.

"It's no good, is it?" he said. "We're not going to find it."

The first spots of rain landed on our heads. I slipped my backpack off my shoulders and began to pull out my rain gear. He slumped to his knees, doing the same, letting the map flutter away as he accidentally pulled out his whistle with his gear.

Then it's as if he's gone wild.

He's blowing the whistle until the muscles bulge out of his neck, letting out his frustration, before jumping to his feet and throwing the thing as far as he can.

It clatters against the rocks. It seems to calm him down.

Slowly he gets to his feet. "Better get it. Axelmann'll do me otherwise."

As he goes off I catch up with the map. Yeandle's cross for marker F stares out at me.

That's when Tozer yells.

"Here! Over here!"

He's standing almost with his nose against the rocks. At least that's what it looks like until I reach him. Then I see what he's found.

There's a slit in the rock, barely head high. It's impossible to see face on, like the join between a pair of stage curtains, but in looking for his whistle Tozer's found it.

"In there," he's saying. "I bet it's a cave. I bet that scummer Axelmann's stuck it in there."

He's inching his way toward the entrance. It's actually beneath us, the ground forming a sort of chute, which slopes down to the gap in the rock wall and on through it.

I grab his arm. "No, Tosh. It's too dangerous. You don't know what it's like in there."

He doesn't want to listen, he's too wound up.

"That marker's in there. I know it's in there. I'm going in . . ."

It was only the furious screech of the whistle that stopped him.

"Greg!" spits Tozer, backing out again. "It's Greg, isn't it? I bet he's come looking for us!"

I don't get a chance to answer.

As we both spin around, he's stomping toward us, white with rage, map fluttering in his hand.

"What the hell are you two doing here? Everybody else has been back for ages. If I hadn't heard your whistle I'd never have found you!"

Tozer's furious, frustrated whistle.

"We wanted to find the marker," mumbles Tozer. "Didn't want to leave till we'd found it." He points at the slit in the rock. "I reckon it's in there."

"In there?" he snarls. "Are you mad?"

As he speaks there's another enormous flash of lightning. The thunder comes an instant later, rolling around us like we're inside a drum. And then the fat blobs of rain start falling.

He looks up at the sky, and his scowl is as dark as the clouds above Ebbor Down. Our leader, our wonderful leader, isn't wearing any rain gear. The half-empty backpack he's wearing shows he isn't carrying any with him either.

Now he's looking around for shelter. There's a solitary tree not far away, but another mighty flash of lightning puts him off going for it. Then the rain starts tipping down as if it's made its mind up to do the job properly, falling in sheets.

That's when he seems to make his mind up too. He

crumples his map into a ball, shoves it into his pocket, then starts toward the entrance in the rock.

"Thought it was in here, did you?" he snaps. "Right, come on."

As the rain falls, we follow him, Tozer in front of me, down the chute and through the slit in the rock.

Out of the wet and into the dry. Out of the warm and into the cool. Out of the light and into the dark.

And, as my foot sinks into the spongy surface, I hear Axelmann say, "Watch out. It's slippery in here."

Chapter 15

"Is he dead yet?" asks Tozer.

He turns his flashlight on, plays its tired beam across the floor at our feet.

I look down at Axelmann's lifeless body, at the jagged rip down one leg of his jogging-suit pants. Then at his top, streaked with mud and slime.

Finally I look down on Axelmann's cold face, at the dark blood staining his swept-back hair. He still hasn't moved or shown any sign of regaining consciousness since it happened.

It had been as if his warning had triggered it all off, although it could only have been our weight. But no sooner had I squeezed through the slit in the rock and heard his voice than the ground seemed to have been pulled away and we were falling, calculations flashing through my mind.

Maybe we landed on top of him. Maybe he hit his head on the rocks as he came down. Maybe the rocks hit him as the floor gave way and the entrance collapsed. I don't know.

Whatever, he's not stirred a fraction since it happened and we took our first terrified look at him.

"I hope he does die," says Tozer.

I bend down, put my fingers against the side of his neck, feeling for his pulse yet again. Thump—thump—thump. It's still there, still firm.

"He's still alive," I say.

"Why hasn't he moved, then? He should have moved after all this time, shouldn't he?"

"It must be a bad concussion."

"Concussion? Boxers get that, don't they?"

"When they get knocked out. Yes."

Tozer's voice is flat, uncaring. "Boxers die from that sometimes, don't they." It's a statement, not a question. "After they've been knocked out."

"If it's bad. If they've damaged their brain and it bleeds inside."

"I hope he's damaged his. I hope he dies. I hate him."

Around the backpack we put under Axelmann's head there's now a small dark pool of liquid, like a dirty halo. In the poor light from Tozer's flashlight I can't tell if it's water or blood or a mix of both. I think it's water. I'm sure the bleeding's stopped. There's been water dripping in all the time.

Tozer aims his flashlight full in Axelmann's face. The weak light makes him look even paler.

"I hate him," says Tozer again. "The way he calls

me Monkey. The way he gets them all laughing at me."

"What?"

Heads swivel around. Laughing heads, all looking toward Tozer. And what's he doing? He's sitting there grinning, pleased with life.

I stare up at him. "But—you always laugh. I've seen you. If you hate it, why do you always laugh?"

Tozer waves his arm angrily toward Axelmann.

"What am I supposed to do? Cry? Run off home and cry about it? Mommy, Mommy, Mr. Axelmann's been calling me names again!"

Can't you see they're laughing at you? Don't you care?

"You don't have to take it, though. Why don't you say something back to him?"

Again his answer stuns me.

"Why do you think? Because I'm thick. Stupid. Because I don't know *what* to say to him."

As I kneel there, he bends down, put his face close to Axelmann's, stares hard at Axelmann's closed eyelids.

"God, I hate you," he breathes. "I hate you."

Tozer stays like that for maybe ten seconds. Then he eases himself back, stands up, looks up at the hopeless gap between us and the hole in the rock wall, up even higher at the shaft of murky light coming in from the outside world.

"Still. Don't matter much now, does it? Don't reckon he'll be calling me it again."

I had no idea. I'd never have believed Tozer hated him so much.

And now I look down at Axelmann's cold face and I'm wondering what *I* think of him—really think of him.

Do I hate you, Axelmann? Do I?

I hate his style. I've hated it this week, for sure. And I hate—yes, and I hate, have always hated deep down, the way he doesn't try to understand people like Tozer, who don't deserve to be treated like clowns even if they act like one.

But do I hate you for not trying to understand me? No.

Why should I? I don't understand me, so why should anybody else—Mom, Dad, you—be able to?

The floor of the pit is getting wetter, muddier. There's a solid trickling of water coming in now, coursing in rivulets down the walls from above.

"Should we try to move him?" I ask. "He's getting soaked."

"Nowhere to move him to, is there?" he says.

Tozer's right. There's now a thin sheet of water across the floor, surrounding us. Axelmann's in the middle, like he's an island.

Tozer turns away again, his boots squelching in the mud. I hear the small rattle as he pulls my whistle from his pocket, brace myself for the shriek.

Putting it between his lips he blows, hard, like a referee blowing for time. As the sound fades, we look up again toward the shaft of dull light, our eyes searching for the slightest hint of movement.

Tozer waits for a second, then lets the whistle fall from his lips.

"They're not coming, are they?" He sounds as if he's lost hope.

I try to raise his spirits. Mine too. "They must be. We've just got to hang on. They'll be here soon."

He swings around on me, his voice a mix of fear and confusion.

"Then why haven't they come by now?" he says. "Your friend, Lonnie. Why hasn't he come? Axie must have told him where he was going."

I look at Axelmann lying at my feet, silent. Then I suddenly remember what he shouted at us.

"What the hell are you two doing here? Everybody else has been back for ages. If I hadn't heard your whistle I'd never have found you!"

I play it over again in my mind, wishing it was telling me something different.

I'd never have found you.

But there's no way out. There's only one conclusion. I can hear my voice shaking as I tell Tozer, not knowing how he's going to take it.

"They're not coming," I say finally.

"What?"

"They didn't know where Axelmann was going."

"What are you on about? He was looking for us. He must have told them he was coming here."

"No. He didn't. Because he couldn't. Remember what he said? 'If I hadn't heard your whistle I'd never have found you.' He *was* looking for us, Tosh. But not here."

Tozer's voice rises, trying to climb above the fear he's feeling—the fear we're both feeling.

"You said I got it right! The compass! Marker F. You said we were in the right place on the map . . ."

Greg's map. Dot to dot. Heart shaped.

I see Greg Yeandle handing the map to me, no-teeth smile. I remember what went through my mind at the time.

Heart-shaped pattern. Seen the right way up, the pattern looks slightly different, seems to have a bit more of a bulge on the side we're going to be following.

My hand's shaking as I pull it out of my pocket, look at it again in the dull light of Tozer's flashlight, remember Yeandle's last words to us.

"See you at the last marker. Don't get lost, now!"

"He's sent us to the wrong place."

"What? What you saying?"

"Greg. He sent us to the wrong place. That's why we didn't find marker F. It was never here."

Another memory, from just before we came in here. Axelmann, crumpling his map into a ball, shoving it into his pocket.

I bend down, start scrabbling through Axelmann's

pockets. It's there, the outside of the ball wet, but the inside still dry and readable.

It's the proof. Axelmann's map has got all the markers laid out on it, every one, every marker that any squad would have had to head for.

Marker F isn't where we are. Yeandle's sent us to the wrong place.

As he sees it, Tozer turns away, hammers his fist against the rock wall again and again, swearing until he's spent.

"Why?" I ask. "Why would he do that?"

"Greg? Why'd you think? Obvious, ain't it? Axie said we had no chance of winning top squad, didn't he?"

"We can't win best squad now. You're going to pay for that, Danny-boy."

"That's why he did it," says Tozer. "For a laugh."

For a while there's a silence neither of us can fill. Then he says, "Greg won't leave us in trouble. He'll tell them where we are."

I swing around on him. Can't he see?

"But he *didn't* tell them, did he? *'Everybody else has been back for ages,'* that's what Axelmann said. He only came looking for us when we didn't show up. And if he wasn't looking for us here, then Greg *couldn't* have told him where he'd sent us."

"He might have told one of the others after. Redrow. Lomax. Your friend Lonnie."

"You think so? Really?"

"No." Tozer gives a shuddering sigh. "And he won't. Like he didn't own up to dropping one of your boots in the lake, just let me take the rap for it."

He looks at me, the pale light from his flashlight dimmer than ever. "We've had it, ain't we?"

I'm still searching for the words, something to say that will give him hope, give me hope, when from above us comes a low, insistent, rumbling noise.

Thunder, but not thunder.

A rumbling like we'd heard before, of rock moving across rock. Except that this time it was louder, building to a peak.

And then the water came.

Chapter 16

"Daniel, the water can come off the Down and into those caves with a power more frightening than you've ever seen. Water, angry water, knowing where its level is and letting nothing stand in its way."

Even as the torrent hits us, Lonnie's words flash into my mind and I can see what's happened.

Water, coming off the Down.

Starting with the storm clouds, then pouring onto the earth in the sheets of rain that had caused Axelmann to pull us in here for shelter in the first place.

Water joining water, drops with drops, rivulets with rivulets, gathering power and strength as it courses downward along the cracks and crevices. Converging on this place, its usual route, and finding its way blocked by the muck and rock that our accident had put in its way.

Pushing, pushing—just as it must have done in prehistoric times, odd drips getting through, then building up to a trickle, pushing and pushing until the blockage couldn't hold out any longer and the water wins its fight.

"Water, angry water, knowing where its level is and letting nothing stand in its way."

It hits Tozer first. The avalanche of mud and water knocks him off his feet and sends him staggering back against the side of our pit. Somehow he manages to hang on to his flashlight.

Then it hits me. For a few seconds, all I can see in the dim light is the white water, pouring down from above us. It's all I can hear, all I can feel.

Instinct takes over. I don't know why, don't know how, but in the middle of the chaos I reach out and fumble for my backpack.

Right for life.

Already the water's seeping through the canvas as I snatch out my flashlight and stuff it inside my jacket. Then Tozer's shouting, waving his flashlight from where he is, backed against the rock across from me.

"Over here!"

The water's not hitting him now. It's still pouring into our pit, but it's like a waterfall, tipping down onto the same spot, and he's crouching out of its line of fire.

I see the water's already up to his ankles. I can feel it's up to mine.

I start to move toward him, then see the figure at my feet—Axelmann, spray cascading over him, still not moving. Already the water's creeping over his chest, half burying his head.

"Axelmann," I shout. "We've got to get him up!"

"Leave him!" screams Tozer, wild-eyed.

"He'll drown!"

"Leave him!"

"We can't leave him!"

Still the water comes, rising, rising. I bend down at Axelmann's head.

For an instant I wonder why my knees feel cold but not wet, then realize it's because I'm wearing waterproof pants.

I try to lift Axelmann's head up, keep his nose and mouth above the rising water.

"Help me, Tosh! Help me!"

"Leave him! Leave him!"

"No!"

The water thunders down, mud and silt coming with it, slapping past us as it falls. Tozer sloshes across to me then, making silly little waves with his feet. He bends down, grabs my hands and tries to drag them away from Axelmann's head.

"We've gotta leave him!" he screams.

Drown, Axelmann, drown!

"We can't leave him!"

"We can!" screams Tozer. "He deserves it! He's scum!"

Drown, Axelmann, drown!

As Tozer yells this, I look down at Axelmann, see

him on the viaduct, hear him in my mind, ranting at Lonnie about me.

"You know what they call him? Do you? Know what they think of him?"

I swing around on Tozer. "So he's scum! But I'm not! We're not!"

He looks at me, hard.

Then he stands up, leaves me to it.

Still the water comes, cascading down. Now it's swirling around Axelmann's head, angry, as if it agrees with Tozer. I push my arm behind the back of Axelmann's limp neck, lever his head up so that his nose and mouth are clear.

It's not enough. I can feel the water rising by the second. It's up to his chin again. I bend lower, try to push one of my arms behind his back as I pull him forward with the other.

It's no good. He's too heavy. I manage to heave him halfway up, but no more. He's slipping. And then Tozer's wading across, saying nothing as he kneels down opposite me and pushes one strong arm down behind Axelmann's back.

We link hands and haul Axelmann into a sitting position.

And still the water comes.

It's roaring and crashing about us, making so much noise I have to shout to make Tozer hear me.

"Take his shoulders!"

"What?"

"We've got to get him floating. I'll hold his legs."

Tozer, hair plastered against his forehead with the wet, shifts himself around behind Axelmann's head. He grips him tightly under the shoulders, just as he'd done to help carry me off the viaduct.

As he heaves, Axelmann's chest comes out of the water. At the same time, I move to his legs and pull them upward. The water takes them, its strength pushing under them, helping me.

And still it comes.

The level's up to my waist now, midthigh on Tozer. Soon we'll be out of our depth.

"Kick your boots off!" I shout.

"Why?"

"You can't swim with them on."

A sudden, stupid thought comes to me. I've known—been avoiding—Tozer for ten years, and I don't know if he can swim.

"You can swim, can't you?"

"Yeh. Not as good as you." He nods wildly down at Axelmann, floating in his arms. Panic shows in his eyes. "Not good enough to hold him up and all!"

"We can't let him go."

"What if it don't stop?" he yells. "What if it don't stop?"

Suddenly there's another low rumble and more lumps of limestone and mud fall from the roof, narrowly missing us as they thump into the water and plow to the bottom. More light comes in, but the same goes for the water as the torrent increases at once, roaring through the extra gap it's just made, pounding down even harder, water on water.

"I'm gonna have to let him go!" shouts Tozer again.

"No!"

"I'm gonna have to! He'll drag me under!"

I look down at Axelmann, see his jogging-suit bulging slightly with trapped air as the water surges around him.

And then my uncontrollable mind is away again, at the lake this time, diving for my boots, finding the first, finding the second bobbing beneath the jetty.

When is a boot like a pair of trousers? When it's got an air pocket. Ha-ha.

"Hang on to him!" I shout, letting Axelmann's legs sink. Then, as quickly as I can, I take my pants off.

It might work. It should work.

I tie a knot at one ankle, then a knot at the other, as Tozer stares at me as if I'm mad.

It must work.

Then, opening out the waist, I plunge the pants under the water as hard as I can.

Yes!

The pants legs fill up with trapped air, swelling out like a couple of sausages. Underneath the water, I'm holding the waistband closed tight.

"Water wings!" I shout.

And then I'm laughing, laughing and crying all at the same time, letting out the fear in one uncontrollable rush.

Seconds later Tozer's doing the same, laughing, crying, shouting, "Ride 'em, Axie!" at the top of his voice as we lay Axelmann's head back between the sausage legs.

"You are something else, Weirdo!" he yells.

This time, I know it's a compliment.

Axelmann's floating. Tozer's balancing against the wall with one hand, still clutching his fading flashlight, hanging on to Axelmann with the other. I'm keeping the air in the makeshift float and treading water, unable to touch the floor of our pit now.

We can keep him up for a while, but not for too much longer.

Still the water comes, faster, faster, pushing us upward.

Pushing us upward.

I look across at Tozer, then above his head, to the gaping hole in the rock wall that he tried to reach before.

Then, it was impossible. But soon . . .

As the torrent pours in, I no longer see the water as our enemy. It's our friend, lifting us, lifting us.

It's more than that.

It's our only hope.

"I can reach it!"

Tozer's shout, cutting through the roar of the water carrying us upward, is what I've been praying for.

The hole in the wall, the passageway the water would have been flowing down if we hadn't blundered into this place . . .

It's our one hope.

We can't keep Axelmann afloat long enough to stand any chance of reaching the entrance, the way we came in. Even if we could, the power of the water would stop us getting him out that way.

But if we can get up to that passageway, get Axelmann into it . . . maybe there'll be another way out. To the lake. We must be near the lake.

That's why this place is called Combe Warren, Daniel. Those rocks over there look strong, but inside them it's like a rabbit warren . . .

"I think I can get up there," shouts Tozer.

Above him, I can see the jagged limestone lip. Tozer's let his flashlight go. Now he's stretching up, clutching the lip with the fingers of his right hand, his left still looped under Axelmann's arm to help keep him afloat.

"Can you hold him?" he shouts.

"I don't know. I think so."

"What do you want me to do, then?"

The water's thundering in. Soon it will be up to the level of the passageway, pouring down it like it's been wanting to all along. If there is another way out, we're going to have to find it quickly. The sooner we get up there the better.

"Go for it!" I shout back.

As Tozer lets go, I swear I hear Axelmann groan. But before I can look at his face, it's gone, sinking under the boiling water as Tozer's support disappears.

Desperately I let go of our makeshift float, use both my hands to pull his head clear, kick hard to stop him dragging me under. This time he does groan, I'm certain of it.

Near me, Tozer's gasping with the effort of trying to heave himself out of the water.

"I can't hold him!" I scream.

Axelmann's body, weighed down by his sodden clothes, is too much. He's pulling me under.

"Hang on!" I hear Tozer shout. "I'm nearly there!"

I just have time to register that Tozer's shout came from above me. Then I go under, hear nothing but the roaring of the water in my ears.

Again I kick, forcing Axelmann's head up to the surface once more. But my strength is going.

Does a drowning man really come up for air three times?

The water's closing over my head again.

And then, suddenly, the weight lifts. Axelmann's body is still there, but it's no longer a millstone pulling me down.

"I got him!"

In the dim light I see Tozer's dumb, wonderful face above my head. He's managed to get himself out. Lying full length in the passageway, he's reached down and grabbed Axelmann under the arms again.

"Turn him around," shouts Tozer.

Between us, we maneuver Axelmann around so that he's facing the wall. After his earlier groans he doesn't make a sound, as if he's thought about regaining consciousness and decided against it.

Tozer grips him under both armpits but doesn't try to pull him up.

"Okay, I've got him," shouts Tozer above the roaring water. "Now you get out."

The water level's about a foot below the lip of the passageway. I reach up with my arms, scrabble with my bare feet on the rock wall, feel the solid shape of the flashlight inside my sodden jacket as I heave myself up and out.

Behind me, the water's still pouring into the pit.

In front of me the passageway looks black and endless.

I turn back to the pit, kneel beside Tozer. He's still holding Axelmann steady.

"You take one arm," he says.

I do it, as he shifts his grip to the other. "We got to bob him up and down, right? Pull when I say so."

He starts counting. "One . . . two . . . three . . ."

With each number we lean out, lowering Axelmann

into the water then pulling him up again, letting the water help us.

"Pull!"

Both gasping with the effort, we heave Axelmann up and halfway out, hooking him over the lip of the passageway like a question mark.

And he groans.

Tozer hears it, looks down at Axelmann, his face a mask.

"Okay," he says, breathing deeply. "On three again. One . . . two . . ."

Maybe it's due to the effect of the cold water, forcing his brain to respond. Who knows? But at that instant Axelmann groans again, lifts his head.

His eyes flick open.

I see the incomprehension and fear flash into them as his mind struggles with what's happening, see them look up at Tozer.

And then I feel Tozer loosen his grip.

Chapter 17

I feel Axelmann's weight pull against my arms as he begins to slide backward.

Drown, Axelmann, drown! He's going to let him drown!

"Tosh, no!"

" . . . three!" screams Tozer.

He's not going to let him drown. He never was.

Beside me, I realize that Tozer hadn't let Axelmann go at all. He'd been reaching out to grab his saturated jogging-suit top in his fist, and now he's pulling, pulling with all his might.

I do the same on my side, but Tozer's the one making all the difference, his face taut with the effort. And then Axelmann's over the lip and into the passageway, lying between us, shuddering and moaning but not trying to move.

Behind him, in the pit, the water is still cascading down. It lands on something, forces it down again every time it bobs up, like a cork under a bath tap.

"My notebook," I say, to myself really.

"What?" says Tozer.

"Nothing. Just my notebook," I say again, pointing. "It was in my backpack."

Tozer looks—at it, then at me.

"Yeh," is all he says.

Then he's bending his head down, close to Axelmann's ear, shouting at him. "You gotta get up!"

Axelmann doesn't move. All I can see is the rise and fall of his breathing.

Again Tozer shouts, as loud as he can, "You gotta get up! Can you hear me? You gotta get up! We gotta move!"

As Tozer's words sink in, some instinct for survival begins to drive Axelmann. He moans, tries to get up onto his knees, doesn't manage it. As he tries again, Tozer lifts Axelmann's arm around his shoulders and helps him to his feet like a wounded soldier.

"Okay," he says to me.

I pull my flashlight out from inside my jacket and click it on, shine its strong beam down into the passageway. Ahead the ground is damp and slippery, the walls glistening with moisture.

There's no sign of any other way out. All we can do is go on.

I move forward, playing the flashlight across the ground and around the walls as we go. The passageway's high enough but narrow, too narrow for me to help Tozer support Axelmann. I look around to check they're still behind me. Axelmann seems to be half conscious, opening and closing his eyes.

We've gone about a hundred feet when the passageway suddenly slopes downward, not steeply, but impossible not to notice.

"Not down. Not down."

It's Axelmann, his voice slurred as if he's drunk.

"You want to go back?" snaps Tozer.

Perhaps he sees in his mind what I do in mine— the water in the pit, rising toward the passageway entrance, like a jug about to overflow. Maybe Tozer's words don't register at all. Whatever, he doesn't argue, not then. He just leans on Tozer and lets himself be led on.

The slope is still going down. Now the roof is getting lower, so that I'm crouching as I go forward.

What are we in?

Odd mathematical shapes dart in and out of my mind.

A tube? A cone? God, don't let us be in a cone!

From behind me come the sounds of Tozer and Axelmann, Tozer panting with effort, Axelmann making odd whimpering noises, as if he's in pain.

And, behind them, the sounds of the water as still it cascades into the place we've just left. Drumming, rumbling sounds, echoing their way down the passageway as if we're playing a game of hide-and-seek and it's warning us that soon it'll be coming, ready or not.

Ahead, the roof is even lower, the gap narrower. I stop, go down on my knees, shine my flashlight through. To call it a passageway is too grand. It's a tunnel, no more, like the long neck of a bottle.

Tozer and Axelmann stop behind me, Axelmann's breath coming in short, sharp gasps.

"Now what?" says Tozer.

"You hang on. I'm going through."

I crawl forward, holding the flashlight out ahead of me. The stretch immediately ahead looks level, but if it gets any narrower there'll be no way through.

As I go, I try to estimate how far I've traveled, put it into footsteps. Thirty feet, not much more.

Suddenly the tunnel looks as if it's come to a dead end. Only as the light from the flashlight bounces back from the wall in front of me do I realize the tunnel's bending, turning a corner. I follow it around, then back again, still on my knees, as the line of the passage straightens up. Am I imagining it, or is it wider now? Higher now?

Suddenly I can lift up. Within a few feet, I can switch from a crawl to a squat, then from a squat to a knees-bent crouch.

And then I'm out, out of the twisting bottleneck and into what seems to be a long, deep chamber. Before I get the chance to play the flashlight around, Tozer's voice comes echoing down the passageway.

"Daniel, you there? Can you hear me?"

I kneel down, shout back. "Yes. I can hear you. I'm out."

Tozer's voice floats back. "You okay?"

"Fine. It's not too far."

I think of telling him how many feet, then say instead, "It'll take you about half a minute. I'll shine the flashlight down from this end. The passage twists in the middle, so you probably won't see it for a while."

I wait, and listen.

Faintly I hear Tozer telling Axelmann, "You better go first."

Then Axelmann, still sounding half awake, half there. "I can't. I can't."

"You can. Daniel's there at the other end. Look for the light."

"I can't."

"You can—sir."

Their voices stop then, to be replaced by muffled sounds of breathing, crawling, getting louder as they come toward me.

Then, suddenly, Axelmann screams in panic as he reaches the twist in the passage and thinks it's a dead end. "Go back! Got to go back!"

"Keep going! Head for the light."

"No light—no light there."

Tozer's voice, hard as iron. "There is. Daniel's there. Keep going."

I wave the flashlight from side to side, finally see

Axelmann's head appear, see him turn in the passage as from behind him I hear Tozer say again, "Keep going."

Then Axelmann's crawling toward me, still crawling even when he gets closer and there's more room to play with. He stays on his knees, shuddering and moaning, until Tozer follows him out of the passage and he can get up and lean on him for support.

"How long we got?" says Tozer.

I've been wondering that myself. The roar of the water has changed, dropped in pitch to a low rumble, as if the jug's nearly full.

"Not long."

Tozer looks over my shoulder, to whatever's behind me. "Then we'd better guess right, eh?"

In the torchlight he's seen what I haven't. The chamber we've ended up in has got not one, but two passageways leading out of it.

The first is off to the side. The second, slightly larger, its roof higher, is straight ahead of us.

"That one," mumbles Axelmann, trying to shuffle toward the one straight ahead, trying to drag Tozer with him.

I go forward and shine the flashlight into it. The beam lights up the first few feet, showing the ground rising upward.

"That way," says Axelmann again, gasping with the effort. "Goes up." Again he tries to drag Tozer forward.

"What d'you reckon?" asks Tozer, looking at me.

"I don't know."

I play the flashlight into the passageway again. The walls are gleaming wet, the floor's the same. But there's something about it, something my mind is wrestling with but can't pin down.

"Up," says Axelmann from deep in his throat. "Up to the top."

"Wait."

I go back the few steps to the other passageway, the one at the side of the chamber, shine the flashlight into that. It looks the same, wet walls, wet ground, except that the floor of the passageway slopes down, heading off farther, deeper into the rabbit warren.

And still my mind is wrestling, still trying to get a hold on something.

"It's coming!"

Axelmann's terrified scream makes me swing around. Water is streaming out of the narrow tunnel, flowing into the chamber. The jug is full.

In a few minutes the tide will be chasing us, after us again.

"Daniel, the water can come off the Down and into those caves with a power more frightening than you've ever seen. Water, angry water, knowing where its level is and letting nothing stand in its way."

"Come on," says Tozer, trying to hide the panic bubbling inside him. "Which way we going? Which way!"

"Up!" screams Axelmann, pulling at Tozer's arm even as it holds him up, his bleary brain telling him to go where his legs haven't got the strength to take him.

And what's my brain telling me? Nothing. Nothing. I can't move.

As I stand there, the water's spurting out of the tunnel even faster, and all I can think of are Lonnie's words.

"Water, angry water, knowing where its level is and letting nothing stand in its way."

It's spreading out into the chamber like a plague. Faster and faster it comes, gushing in, eddying around, fingers of water probing into both the passageways.

I see it flow into the one beside me, bubbling as it slips away.

Tozer and Axelmann are straight ahead, ready to go into that passageway. It's as if they're standing on the beach with the tide coming in. The water's swirling around their feet, little splashes jumping into the air as the flow coming back down the slope meets the water trying to fight its way up.

"Which way, Daniel!"

Water, angry water, knowing where its level is . . .

At that instant, I know the answer, bless my weird and wonderful mind for giving it to me.

"This way!"

I'm pointing into the passageway at my side, the water now coursing down it ever more rapidly.

Tozer starts to move toward me, but Axelmann pulls him back.

"No!" he slurs. "No! This one. Up!"

"That way's no good," I shout. "It's a dead end. Look!"

Tozer stares at me, not understanding. I splash up to him, flash the flashlight deep into the passageway Axelmann wants to enter. There's water trying to flow up, reaching a new high point as we watch. But above it, there's no water trying to come down. No water trying to find its level.

"Rain, Tosh. It flows off Ebbor Down. If that was a way out, there'd be water coming down it. But there isn't!"

Tozer pauses, looks, just for a couple of seconds. Then, to Axelmann. "We're going the way Daniel says."

"No!" Axelmann's pulling at Tozer, panic fueling his strength. "Got to go up! He's wrong. He's wrong. Got to go up."

Tozer's struggling to hold him.

"You've got to take me up! Help me, Monkey. Take me up!"

That's when Tozer hits him.

Hard, with the flat of his hand, on the side of Axelmann's face. The sound of it rings around the chamber.

Axelmann looks at Tozer, stunned, disbelieving. His lips move, but no words come out.

"I trust him," says Tozer. "So you trust him."

As he says it, Axelmann seems to crumble. His eyes fade, as if the light has been turned off behind them. With a shudder he slumps against Tozer, doesn't try to resist as Tozer leads him down the passageway after me.

It's hard going. The floor is pitted and rutted. We stumble along, feeling the water pressing up against the backs of our legs, seeing it rush past us.

There's nothing to say. I'm in front, shining the flashlight ahead, trying to give them as much warning of the twists and turns of the passageway as I can.

Behind me I can hear Tozer's voice, steady and firm, and he helps Axelmann along. "One o'clock . . . twelve o'clock . . . two o'clock . . ."

The roar of the water is growing ever louder as more and more floods into the chamber we've left behind, then sets off to chase after us.

It's getting higher. Knee high, deeper than that as the passageway dips into hollows and comes out again. Ahead, the walls are glistening in the flashlight beam as spray bounces up onto them, then streams off again to continue its downward course.

Down. We're still going down.

Suddenly, Axelmann falls. I stop, do what I can to help Tozer as he struggles to get him to his feet again. Axelmann's face is a blank.

We go on, now with one of Axelmann's arms around my shoulders. His legs are moving, but it feels as if he's taking hardly any of his own weight. We're carrying him. How Tozer's managed to get him this far I don't know. He looks whacked.

Around another corner. The water surges up the sides of the passageway like it's a wall of death, lashing at us as it goes.

And there's the noise. The noise has been deafening, rolling around us, bouncing down from the rocks.

So why does it seem to be getting quieter?

Axelmann lurches to Tozer's side as we reach another turn in the passageway and a wave of water hits us from behind.

Beside me, I hear Tozer give a shout of pain.

I watch the torrent race away, bubbling and boiling in the beam from my flashlight, watch it race away—then disappear.

Disappear as if it's been sliced off by a razor.

And then I realize that Tozer's shout wasn't one of pain, but a shout of joy.

I realize that the water's disappearing because it's falling off the end of the passageway.

That it's reached its level.

Realize that, above it, I can see a ribbon of blue sky.

Chapter 18

"How is he?" I ask.

Lonnie does his usual, glances at me then looks out across the lake.

"Your Mr. Axelmann? Physically, not bad. A fair few bumps and bruises. Still pretty badly concussed. They're keeping him in for another day at least. You won't have the pleasure of his company on the bus home, I'm afraid."

He turns back to me. "How about you, Daniel? How are you?"

I turn Lonnie's way, answer his question. "Fine. I'm fine."

He nods, as if I don't need to say any more, but waiting in case I want to.

It's my turn to look across the lake now. Up on Ebbor Down it's all blue sky and fluffy clouds, as if it's resting after yesterday's storm. Beneath, as they drop to the lakeside, the dark limestone walls seem to flash signals at us as the sun catches the water still trickling out.

I think I can see where we came out, but I'm not sure. Already the memories are starting to blur . . .

In the passageway, wading, running the final few steps toward the ribbon of sky. Clambering out, trying to find a decent footing on the rocks without being knocked flying by the escaping water. Seeing the jetty far away and realizing where we were.

Leaving Tozer, exhausted Tozer, to stay with the shivering Axelmann while I found my way around the lakeside and raised the alarm.

Sirens, ambulances, more passageways—antiseptic this time—then the doctors, the nurses, the questions, the tests. And the hospital bed and the feel of the crisp dry sheets. Oh, how dry!

Mr. Redrow came in with us. As I'm lying there, I hear him ask if he can use the telephone. For some reason it just doesn't occur to me who he might be calling, not until I hear him say, "Hello. Mr. Edwards . . ."

I pick up snatches of what Redrow's telling Dad— "orienteering exercise . . . went the wrong way . . . trapped underground . . . three of them . . ." It's not too difficult working out what's being said at the other end of the line.

Not, that is, until I hear Redrow use a tone of voice that'll work wonders if he ever tries it in class.

"Mr. *Edwards.* I don't think you *understand.* With-out Daniel and the other boy. . ."

He lowers his voice at that point and I don't really

catch anything more he says, except that he keeps his new teacher tone throughout.

Then it all goes quiet. I think he's hung up, but he hasn't. The next thing I know he's handing me the telephone.

"Your father. I've told him what happened."

I take it. As Redrow tiptoes out I mutter, "Hello?"

"Danny? Danny, it's Dad. You all right?"

"Fine."

"Your teacher—Redruth, is it?"

"Redrow."

"Redrow. He's just told me what happened. I said we'd come and get you. Leave as soon as your mom comes home—she's out, see? But he reckons they want to keep you in the hospital for the night anyway and as you're coming back tomorrow . . . look, you sure you're all right? We can be there in a couple of hours if I put my foot down."

"It's okay. I'm fine now."

The line goes quiet for a moment. Then he says, "I got the wrong end of the stick for a while. Thought what had happened was all your . . ." He doesn't finish the sentence, just starts another one, almost to himself at first. "Typical. Anyway. The way Redrow tells it, this teacher Axelmann wouldn't have made it if it hadn't been for you."

"There were two of us, Dad."

"Right. But . . ." It's as if he's run out of words for

the first time in his life. "Look . . . see you tomorrow, yeh? We'll be there to meet the bus. Okay?"

"Yes. See you then."

The line goes quiet again, and I think he's hung up. I'm just about to put the receiver down when he says, "Daniel?"

"Yes?"

"Love you, son."

And then he's gone, those three words overtaken so quickly by the purr of the dial tone that now, as I look out across the lake, I'm starting to wonder if I really heard them. The low sound of the bus horn comes through the trees.

Beside me, Lonnie says, "Time you were going."

I don't move at first. There's one memory that hasn't started to blur, one that I could see clearly every time I closed my eyes in that hospital bed. The look I saw on Axelmann's face when Tozer hit him.

"Axelmann," I say to Lonnie. "You said 'physically, not bad.' What about . . . ?"

"Mentally? I don't know, Daniel. I think he found out a few things about himself yesterday, down there."

"We all did."

"Sure. But you, and Tozer, found out some good things about yourselves. Axelmann didn't. He found out a lot about himself he didn't like. That part's going to stay with him a lot longer than his bruises."

As another blast comes from the bus horn I take a

final look at the lake, then turn away. Lonnie walks with me, whistling quietly.

Ask him. You want to know, you know you do. Ask him.

"Lonnie. Can I ask you something? Personal?"

"Sure." That contented smile. "If I don't want to answer I can always tell you to jump in the lake."

As he laughs, I feel that I could ask this man anything. And what I want to know isn't much.

"Why do you like to be called 'Lonnie'?" I ask.

I feel, rather than see, him glance my way. "Like I told you all. It's what my mom called me."

"But why?"

He stops then, turns back to point toward the jetty and the waters of the lake. "Because of all the time I used to spend down there on my own. Swimming, fishing—often no more than tossing in stones of different sizes. 'Always watching the water,' she'd say. 'Happy on your own, Lonnie alone . . .'"

He puts a hand on my shoulder. "Understand?"

"Yes. I understand."

"Thought you might." He starts walking again. "Come on. They'll be waiting for you."

As I climb on the bus everything goes quiet.

I look around. Greg Yeandle and Flick Harris are at the back again. Neither of them looks up. In the brief inquest there'd been, Yeandle had denied sending us the wrong way deliberately.

"Genuine mistake, sir. Feel gutted about what happened, don't we, Flick?"

The seat I had on the way here is empty. I slide into it.

Outside, beneath me, Mr. Redrow is watching the bus driver load the last of the suitcases. Mr. Lomax hurries up the steps, feeling his pockets for a pen. He finds one, then starts to call the roll.

There's no answer when he calls Tozer's name.

"Tozer? Anybody seen Tozer?"

"Down a hole, sir?"

"That is not funny."

"Think he nipped down to the village shop, sir."

"Yeh, here he comes! Good old Tosher! All behind as usual."

Tozer's loping down the road toward us. In his hand he's clutching a brown paper bag.

The catcalls rise to a peak as he clumps up the steps.

"Back here, Tosher!"

"Saved a seat for you, mate!"

Tozer grins, sticks his thumb up as he looks toward the back. But, as he moves down the aisle, he stops and sits down next to me.

"Hi. How you doing?"

I look at him. We haven't really talked together at all since yesterday, just answered other people's questions about what happened.

"Fine," I say. "You?"

"Okay, I reckon. Evil breakfast in the hospital, weren't it?"

He laughs. I do too.

Neither of us knows what to say next.

"Hear they kept Axie in," he says after a few seconds.

I nod. "At least another day, Lonnie says. More observation."

"Brain scan, maybe. See if he's got one, eh?"

"Or to find out if it's been scrambled."

"Uh?"

"By you. Hitting him."

He grins at the memory. "Right. Yeh. Enjoyed that."

We both fall silent again. From behind us comes another volley of calls.

"Tosher! You coming up here, then?"

"Your seat's getting cold."

Tozer looks around into the aisle, then turns back to me again. He's only half sitting in the seat.

"Think he'll be different to us when he comes back?" he says. "Axie?"

"I think so. I hope so."

"Just hope he don't remember me thumping him!"

I laugh as he adds, "Worth it, though."

We lapse into silence again. This time it's broken by Yeandle's voice, coming from his prime position on the wide rear seat.

"Tosher! You coming, or not?"

Now Flick. "Better company back here."

Then Yeandle again, his voice clear for all to hear. "Come on, Tosher! You know Weirdo prefers it on his own!"

Before I know it Tozer's on his feet, standing in the aisle, jabbing a finger at them.

"Don't call him that! Hear me? Don't you *ever* call him that again!"

Now he's looking around the bus, glaring at everybody else, finger still jabbing. "Any of you!"

Outside, the driver slams down the lid of the luggage compartment.

Inside, there's a stunned silence.

Finally Greg Yeandle says, "Sure. Sure enough, Tosh."

"Thanks," I say as Tozer sits down beside me again.

He shakes his head, says nothing.

Up at the front, Mr. Lomax climbs aboard for a final look around. "Everybody sitting comfortably?" he trills. "I don't want any moving around once we're on the way."

"Hang on, sir. I'm just changing seats."

I look at Tozer.

"Going to the back," he says to me, easing himself out toward the aisle. "With Greg and Flick."

"What?"

He shrugs. "Yeh."

"After what happened? Why?"

"Because I need 'em," he says simply.

I can't believe he's saying it, try to make him see sense.

"You don't need them, Tosh. They just use you. You know they do. They're not real friends, you said so yourself."

"Yeh, I know. But they're all I've got, see?"

He looks down at me, grins the grin I've always thought was dumb because I couldn't see the sadness behind it.

"Reckon brains are a bit like the spuds game, eh? Where you end up depends on what you start with."

He takes a couple of steps down the aisle, then comes back, holds out the brown paper bag he's been cradling.

"Here. To make up for the other one."

I reach out, take the bag from him as he says, "You're all right, Daniel."

And then he's off, heading for the back, and the cheers and hoots are ringing out.

"Tosher!"

"This one, Tosher. Here!"

From the back, I hear Yeandle say, "No hard feelings, Tosher?"

"No harm meant," chips in Flick. "Joke, like."

"Y'know? Bit of a laugh, bit of a giggle . . ."

I open the paper bag.

There's a notebook inside.

Tozer's bought me a notebook.

Around me the babbling begins. I sit back, not hearing them, hearing only the voices of the past week.

"Water finds its level, Daniel, the same way you've got to."

"Love you, son."

"You're all right, Daniel."

The bus judders as the driver starts the engine. I take a last look out of the window, see the summit of Ebbor Down away in the distance.

Now other thoughts begin crowding into my mind, jostling for position.

How high is it? How fast would that water have been coming off it? How much? Is there a formula?

And I open my new notebook at the first page.